Praise for Graham Swift's

Mothering Sunday

"Swift's small fiction feels like a masterpiece. . . .
[He] creat[es] a perfect small tragedy with all the
spring and tension of a short story, spinning around
it a century of consequences with so light a touch
that they only brush against the charmed centre."
—*The Guardian*

"[A] beautiful gem of a novel."
—*The Philadelphia Inquirer*

"An elegant reflection on the impulse to tell stories. . . . A demonstration of what this Booker win-
ner can do in the tight space of a single day."
—*The Washington Post*

"Dazzling. . . . Wonderfully accomplished."
—*The Sunday Times* (London)

"A meditation on and a manifestation of 'a complete fiction.' . . . [*Mothering Sunday*] eloquently
accounts for the beginning of a vocation, and the
re-beginning of an individual."
—*Minneapolis Star Tribune*

"A rare read indeed. . . . For all the detailed exami-
nation of character and the bold sweep of time,
there is not a word wasted."
—*The Spectator* (London)

Graham Swift

Mothering Sunday

Graham Swift was born in 1949 and is the author of ten novels; two collections of short stories; and *Making an Elephant*, a book of essays, portraits, poetry, and reflections on his life in writing. With *Waterland* he won the Guardian Fiction Award, and with *Last Orders* the Booker Prize. Both novels have since been made into films. His work has appeared in more than thirty languages.

INTERNATIONAL

ALSO BY GRAHAM SWIFT

England and Other Stories

Wish You Were Here

Making an Elephant

Tomorrow

The Light of Day

Last Orders

Ever After

Out of This World

Waterland

Learning to Swim

Shuttlecock

The Sweet-Shop Owner

Mothering Sunday

Mothering Sunday

A Romance

Graham Swift

VINTAGE INTERNATIONAL
Vintage Books
A Division Of Penguin Random House LLC
New York

FIRST VINTAGE INTERNATIONAL EDITION, JANUARY 2017

The Library of Congress has cataloged the Knopf edition
as follows:
Names: Swift, Graham, author.
Title: Mothering Sunday : a romance / Graham Swift.
Description: First edition. | New York:
Alfred A. Knopf, 2016
Identifiers: LCCN 2015033402
Subjects: | BISAC : FICTION/Literary. | FICTION/
Historical. | GSAFD : Love stories.
Classification: LCC PR6069.W47 M68 2016 |
DDC 823/.914—dc23
LC record available at
http://lccn.loc.gov/2015033402

**Vintage Books Trade Paperback ISBN: 978-1-101-97172-7
eBook ISBN: 978-1-101-94753-1**

Book design by Cassandra J. Pappas

www.vintagebooks.com

Printed in the United States of America
10 9 8 7 6 5 4

For Candice

You *shall* go to the ball!

Mothering Sunday

ONCE UPON A TIME, before the boys were killed and when there were more horses than cars, before the male servants disappeared and they made do, at Upleigh and at Beechwood, with just a cook and a maid, the Sheringhams had owned not just four horses in their own stable, but what might be called a "real horse," a racehorse, a thoroughbred. Its name was Fandango. It was stabled near Newbury. It had never won a damn thing. But it was the family's indulgence, their hope for fame and glory on the racecourses of southern England. The deal was that Ma and Pa—otherwise known in his strange language as "the shower"—owned the head and body and he and Dick and Freddy had a leg each.

"What about the fourth leg?"

"Oh the fourth leg. That was always the question."

For most of the time it was just a name, never seen, though an expensively quartered and trained name. It had been sold in 1915—when he'd been fifteen too. "Before you showed up, Jay." But once, long ago, early one June morning, they'd all gone, for the strange, mad expedition of it, just to watch it, just to watch Fandango, their horse, being galloped over the downs. Just to stand at the rail and watch it, with other horses, thundering towards them, then flashing past. He and Ma and Pa and Dick and Freddy. And—who knows?—some other ghostly interested party who really owned the fourth leg.

He had a hand on her leg.

It was the only time she'd known his eyes go anything close to misty. And she'd had the clear sharp vision (she would have it still when she was ninety) that she might have gone with him—might still somehow miraculously go with him, just him—to stand at the rail and watch Fandango hurtle past, kicking up the mud and dew. She had never seen such a thing but she could imagine it, imagine it clearly. The sun still coming up, a red disc, over the grey downs, the air still crisp and cold, while he shared with her, perhaps, a silver-capped hip flask and, not especially stealthily, clawed her arse.

BUT SHE WATCHED him now move, naked but for a silver signet ring, across the sunlit room. She would not later in life use with any readiness, if at all, the word "stallion" for a man. But such he was. He was twenty-three and she was twenty-two. And he was even what you might call a thoroughbred, though she did not have that word then, any more than she had the word "stallion." She did not yet have a million words. Thoroughbred: since it was "breeding" and "birth" that counted with his kind. Never mind to what actual purpose.

It was March 1924. It wasn't June, but it was a day like June. And it must have been a little after noon. A window was flung open, and he walked, unclad, across the sun-filled room as carelessly as any unclad animal. It was his room, wasn't it? He could do what he liked in it. He clearly could.

And she had never been in it before, and never would be again.

And she was naked too.

March 30th 1924. Once upon a time. The shadows from the latticework in the window slipped over him like foliage. Having gathered up the cigarette case and lighter and a little silver ashtray from the dressing table, he turned, and there, beneath a nest of dark hair and fully bathed by sunshine, were his cock and balls, mere floppy and still sticky appendages. She could look at them if she liked, he didn't mind.

But then he could look at her. She was stretched out naked, except for a pair—her only pair—of very cheap earrings. She hadn't pulled up the sheet. She had even clasped her hands behind her head the better to look at him. But he could look at her. Feast your eyes. It was an expression that came to her. Expressions had started to come to her. Feast your eyes.

Outside, all Berkshire stretched out too, girded with bright greenery, loud with birdsong, blessed in March with a day in June.

He was still a follower of horses. That is, he still threw money away on them. It was his version of economising, to throw money away. For nearly eight years he'd had money for three, in theory. He called it "loot." But he would show he could do without it. And what the two of them had been doing for almost seven years cost, as he would sometimes remind her, absolutely nothing. Except secrecy and risk and cunning and a mutual aptitude for being good at it.

But they had never done anything like this. She had never been in this bed before—it was a single bed, but roomy. Or in this room, or in this house. If it cost nothing, then this was the greatest of gifts.

Though if it cost nothing, she might always remind him, then what about the times when he'd given her sixpences? Or was it even three-pences? When it was only just beginning, before it got—was it the right word?—serious. But she would never dare remind him. And not now any-way. Or dare throw at him the word "serious."

He sat on the bed beside her. He ran a hand across her belly as if brushing away invisible dust. Then he arranged on it the lighter and ash-tray, retaining the cigarette case. He took two cigarettes from the case, putting one in her own proffered, pouting lips. She had not taken her hands from the back of her head. He lit hers, then his. Then, gathering up the case and lighter to put on the bedside table, he stretched out beside her, the ashtray still positioned halfway between her navel and what these days he would happily, making no bones about it, call her "cunt."

Cock, balls, cunt. There were some simple, basic expressions.

It was March 30th. It was a Sunday. It was what used to be known as Mothering Sunday.

"WELL, you have a gorgeous day for it, Jane," Mr. Niven had said as she brought in fresh coffee and toast.

"Yes, sir," she'd said and she'd wondered quite what he meant by "it" in her case.

"A truly gorgeous day." As if it were something he had generously provided. And then to Mrs. Niven, "You know, if someone had told us it was going to be like this, we might as well have all packed hampers. A picnic—by the river."

He said it wistfully, yet eagerly, so that, putting down the toast rack, she'd thought for an instant there might actually be a change of plan and she and Milly would be required to pack a hamper. Wherever the hamper *was*, and whatever they were supposed to put in it at such inconsiderate notice. This being *their* day.

And then Mrs. Niven had said, "It's March, Godfrey," with a distrusting glance towards the window.

Well, she'd been wrong. The day had only got better.

And anyway the Nivens had their plan, on which the weather could only smile. They were to drive to Henley to meet the Hobdays and the Sheringhams. Given their common predicament—which only occurred once a year and only for a portion of one day—they were all to meet for lunch at Henley and so deal with the temporary bother of having no servants.

It was the Hobdays' idea—or invitation. Paul Sheringham was to marry Emma Hobday in just two weeks' time. So the Hobdays had suggested to the Sheringhams an outing for lunch: an opportunity to toast and talk over the forthcoming event, as well as a solution to Sunday's practical difficulty. And then because the Nivens were close friends and neighbours of the Sheringhams and would be honoured guests at the wedding (and would have the same difficulty), the Nivens—as Mr. Niven had put it to her when first notifying her of these arrangements—had been "roped in."

This had all made clear one thing she knew already. Whatever else Paul Sheringham was marrying, he was marrying money. Perhaps he had to, the way he got through his own. The Hobdays would be paying in two weeks' time for a grand wedding, and did you really need to celebrate a forthcoming celebration? Not unless you had plenty to spare. It might demand nothing less than champagne. When Mr. Niven had mentioned the hamper he had perhaps been wondering how much the Hobdays' liberality could be relied on or how much the day might involve his own pocket.

But that the Hobdays had plenty to spare pleased her. It had nothing to do with her, but it pleased her. That Emma Hobday might be made of five-pound notes, that the marriage might be an elaborate way of obtaining "loot," pleased or, rather, consoled her. It was all the other things it might entail that—even as Mr. Niven explained about the "roping in"—gnawed at her.

And would Mister Paul and Miss Hobday be joining the party themselves? She couldn't really ask it directly, vital as it was to her to know. And Mr. Niven didn't volunteer the information.

"Would you mention these arrangements to Milly? None of it of course need affect—your own arrangements."

It was not often that he had the occasion to say such a thing.

"Of course, sir."

"A jamboree in Henley, Jane. A meeting of the tribes. Let's hope we have the weather for it."

She wasn't quite sure what "jamboree" meant, though she felt she had read the word some-where. But "jam" suggested something jolly.

"I hope so too, sir."

AND NOW they clearly had the weather for it, and Mr. Niven, whatever his earlier misgivings, was indeed getting rather jolly. He was going to be driving himself. He had already announced that they might as well set off soon, so they could "pootle around" and take advantage of such a lovely morning. He wouldn't, apparently, be calling on Alf at the garage, who—for the right sum—could become a convincing chauffeur. In any case, as she'd observed over recent years, Mr. Niven liked driving. He even preferred the pleasure of driving to the dignity of being driven. It gave him a boyish zest. And as he was always saying, with a whole variety of intonations, ranging from bluster to lament, times were changing.

Once upon a time, after all, the Nivens would have met the Sheringhams at Sunday service.

"Tribes" had suggested something hot and outdoors. She knew it was to be the George Hotel in Henley. It was not to be a picnic. And it might well have been a day, since it was still March, of evil gales, even snow. But it was a morning like a morning in summer. And Mrs. Niven left the table to go up to get herself ready.

She couldn't ask, even now with Mr. Niven conveniently alone, "Would Miss Hobday and . . . ?"

Even if it sounded like just a maid's idle curiosity. Wasn't the coming wedding the only current talking-point? And she certainly couldn't ask, "If not, then what other separate arrangements might the two of them have in mind?"

She didn't think that if she were one half of a betrothed couple—or at least Paul Sheringham's half—she would want, two weeks before their wedding, to attend a jamboree in Henley to be fussed over by the older generation (by what he might have called—she could see him speaking with a cigarette in his mouth and wincingly screwing up his eyes—"three bloody showers together").

But in any case, if she got no further information, it still left the problem that was peculiarly hers on this day, as Mr. Niven knew, of what to do with it. Today it was painfully peculiar. The gorgeous weather didn't necessarily help at all. It only seemed—with two weeks to go—to deepen a shadow.

She was going to say to Mr. Niven, when the moment came, that if he—if he and Mrs. Niven— didn't mind, she might not "go" anywhere. She might just stay here at Beechwood and read a book if that was all right—"her book" as she might put it, though it belonged to Mr. Niven. She might just sit somewhere in the sunshine in the garden.

She knew that Mr. Niven could only approve of such a harmless suggestion. He might even think it was a rather appealing image. And of course it would mean she'd be ready to resume her duties at once, whenever they returned. She could find something to eat in the kitchen. Milly, before she left, might even make her a sandwich. She could have her own "picnic."

And it might even have happened just like that. The bench in the nook by the sundial. Bumblebees tricked by the weather. The magnolia tree already loaded with blossom. Her book on her lap. She knew which book it would be.

So—she would put the idea to Mr. Niven.

But then the telephone had rung and—it being one of her numberless duties—she'd hastened to answer it. And her heart had soared. That was a phrase you read in books, but it was sometimes actually true of what happened to people. It was true then of herself. Her heart had soared, like some stranded heroine's in a story. Like the larks she would hear in a little while, trilling and soaring high in the blue sky, as she pedalled her way to Upleigh.

But she'd been careful to say, quite loudly, into the receiver and with her best answering-the-telephone voice that was both maid-like and somewhat queenly, "Yes, madam."

CHURCH BELLS THROBBED beneath the birdsong. Warm air wafted through the open window. He had not drawn the curtains, not even out of token delicacy to her. Delicacy to her? But it wasn't necessary. The room looked out over trees and grass and gravel. The sunshine only applauded their nakedness, dismissing all secrecy from what they were doing, though it was utterly secret.

And they had never been, in all their years of—what to call it? Intimacy? Freedom with each other?—as naked as this.

Feast your eyes, she'd dared to think, like some smuggled-in beauty. Was she a beauty? She had the red knuckles and worn-down nails of her kind. Her hair must have been all over the place. It was stuck to her forehead. Yet she'd even felt something of his imperious immodesty—as if *he* were the servant bringing her a cigarette.

And barely two hours ago she had called *him* "madam"! Since it was his voice down the telephone and, for all her sudden servant-girl giddiness, she had needed to keep her presence of mind. The door to the breakfast room was open. Mr. Niven was still occupied with toast and marmalade. Down the telephone had come quick, terse, undisobeyable instructions, while she'd said, "Yes, madam . . . No, madam . . . That's quite all right, madam."

Her heart had soared. Feast your eyes. A story was beginning.

And less than an hour later, after she'd stepped off her bicycle and he'd opened the front door for her—the front door no less, as if she were a real visitor and he were a head footman—they'd laughed at her calling him "madam." They'd laughed as she'd said it again as he ushered her in. "Thank you, madam." And he'd said, "You're

clever, Jay. Do you know that? You're clever."
That was the way he paid compliments, as if
revealing to her something she might never
have imagined.

But, yes, she was clever. Clever enough to
know she was cleverer than him. She had always,
especially in the early days, out-clevered him.
It was what he wanted, she knew it, to be out-
clevered, even in some strange way commanded.
Though it could never be said of course, or even
suggested. She would never quite erase, even
when she was ninety, her inner curtsey. There
was always the given of his princely authority.
He ruled the roost, didn't he? He'd ruled it now
for nearly eight years. He had the run. He had
the run of her. Oh yes, he was princely. She'd
helped him form the habit.

But he'd called her "clever," as they stood
together in the vestibule, almost with confessing
humility, as if he were the evident fool, the hope-
less case. Outside, bordering the gravel, were
ribbons of brilliant daffodils, and inside, across
the hall, rising from a large bowl, were twists of
almost luminous white flowers. Then the door

had shut behind her, and she was alone with him inside Upleigh House at eleven on a Sunday morning. Something she'd never been before.

"WHO WAS IT, Jane?" Mr. Niven had said. He might have been thinking, from the "madam," that it was Mrs. Sheringham or even Mrs. Hobday with some change of plan.

"Wrong number, sir."

"Really, and on a Sunday," he'd said, rather meaninglessly.

Then, glancing at the clock and furling his napkin, he'd given a ceremonious cough.

"Well, Jane, after you've dealt with the breakfast things, you may go. So may Milly. But before you do—"

And with these words he'd awkwardly produced the half-crown that she knew had been waiting and that merited one of her more pronounced bobbings.

"Thank you, sir. That's very kind of you."

"Well—you have a beautiful day for it," he reiterated, and she wondered again, even a little flusteredly, what he could mean by "it."

But he looked at her only enquiringly, not searchingly. Then he drew himself up, even becoming rather official.

It was a strange business, this Mothering Sunday ahead of them, a ritual already fading, yet the Nivens—and the Sheringhams—still clung to it, as the world itself, or the world in dreamy Berkshire, still clung to it, for the same sad, wishing-the-past-back reasons. As the Nivens and the Sheringhams perhaps clung to each other more than they'd used to, as if they'd become one common decimated family.

It was strange in her case for quite different reasons, and it all elicited from Mr. Niven, as well as the half-crown, much throat-clearing and correctness.

"Milly will take the First Bicycle and leave it at the station for her return. And you, Jane . . . ?"

There were no longer horses, but there were bicycles. The two in question were virtually identical—Milly's had a slightly larger basket—but they were scrupulously known as the "first" and "second" bicycles, and Milly, as befitted her seniority, had the first one.

She herself would have the second one. She might be at Upleigh inside fifteen minutes. Though there was still the matter of formal permission—if not for going to Upleigh.

"If I may, sir, I'll just take myself off. On the Second Bicycle."

"That's what I had been assuming, Jane."

She might have just said "my bicycle," but Mr. Niven was a stickler for the "first" and "second" thing, and she'd learnt to go along with it. She knew, from Milly, that the "boys"—Philip and James—had once had bicycles (as well as horses) which had become known as the First and Second Bicycles. The boys were gone, so were their bicycles, but for some strange reason the "first" and "second" tradition had carried over to the two servants' bicycles, even though these were, necessarily, ladies' versions, without crossbars. She and Milly perhaps didn't qualify as ladies, but they qualified, in one persistent respect, as the dim ghosts of Philip and James.

She had never known Philip and James, but Milly had once known them and indeed cooked for them. And Milly had once known "her lad," who'd gone the same way as Philip and James, even perhaps in the same dreadful part of France. And her lad had been called Billy. Milly would not often use his name—"my lad" had become as obligatory as "first" and "second" bicycles—so it was hard to gauge how much she'd actually, really known him. Yet if they'd ever got married they would have been Milly and Billy. Perhaps "her lad" was a fiction of Milly's that no one could disprove, or would wish to. The war had suited all purposes.

ONCE UPON A TIME . . . Once upon a time she'd arrived, the new maid, Jane Fairchild, at Beechwood just after a great gust of devastation. The family, like many others, had been whittled down, along with the household budget and the servants. Now, there was only a cook and a maid. Cook Milly, with her seniority, had been theoretically promoted to cook and housekeeper, but she clung to the kitchen, while she, the new and inexperienced maid, soon effectively did most of the housekeeping.

She didn't mind any of this. She loved Milly.

Cook Milly was just three years her elder, but it seemed a condition of the loss of "her lad" that she'd rapidly put on weight and girth, even developed an air of scatty wisdom, and so become like the mother she'd perhaps always wanted to be. "Her lad" even began to suggest she might have been the poor boy's mother.

And today Cook Milly, if her bicycle could bear her weight to the station, was going to see her mother.

"OF COURSE you may, Jane," Mr. Niven had said, inserting the napkin into its silver ring. Was he going to ask her where she was thinking of going?

"You have the Second Bicycle at your disposal and you have—ahem—two and six. And you have the whole county at your disposal. As long as you come back again!"

Then, as if slightly envying the broad freedom

he'd just granted, he said, "It's *your* day, Jane. You may be—ahem—at your own devices." He knew, by now, that such a phrase would not be over her head—it might even have been meant as a gentle tribute to her reading habits. Cook Milly might have thought "devices" meant kitchen spoons.

He can't surely have meant anything else by it.

IT WAS March 30th 1924. It was Mothering Sunday. Milly had her mother to go to. But the Nivens' maid had her simple liberty, and half a crown to go with it. Then the telephone had rung, rapidly altering her previous plan. No, she wouldn't be having a picnic.

And it was surely more than she could ever have hoped for, since even if Mister Paul and Miss Hobday were not to be of the Henley party it had left open the question of how they might both pass the day together anyway. A question which still remained open.

They both had cars, she knew this. Young people of their kind could have cars now. He sometimes referred to hers as the "Emma-mobile." They would certainly both be at *their* own devices, and if they played their cards right they might, if it was their inclination, have at their disposal either of two helpfully emptied houses. If you thought about it, up and down the country on this day there might be any number of temporarily vacated houses available for secret assignations. And if she knew Paul Sheringham . . .

Exactly. She knew him and she didn't know him. She knew him in some ways better than anyone—she would always be sure of that—while knowing that no one else must ever know how much she knew him. But she knew him well enough to know the ways in which he was not knowable. She didn't know what he was thinking now, as he lay naked beside her. She often thought he didn't think anything.

She didn't know how he behaved with Emma Hobday. She didn't know how much Emma Hobday—Miss Hobday—knew him. She didn't know Emma Hobday. Having only glimpsed her once or twice, how could she? She knew she was pretty, in a flowery kind of way. She was the kind of woman who might be called a flower, who dressed in flowery clothes. But she had no idea what she was like, as it were, beneath the flowers. How could she? Paul scarcely spoke of her, though he was going to marry her. And that, while it showed her how much she didn't know Paul Sheringham, was a comforting mystery.

What seemed, oddly, to be happening was that the closer Paul Sheringham and Miss Hobday got to marrying, the less time they actually spent in each other's company. She had heard of that thing where brides and grooms weren't supposed to see each other for a day (or was it just a night?) before their wedding, but this was a sort of expanded version of that practice and had been going on for some time. He ought surely to make some stronger show of being the eager husband.

So the phrase had come to her, like a phrase too from a book, that had suddenly acquired actual meaning: "arranged marriage."

It was the best she could hope for. Not that it really helped her. But if, for whatever reason, a combination of flowers and money, he was slipping towards such a thing, then this day—so she had thought even as she attended to breakfast and Mr. Niven spoke about hampers—this day that had begun with such promising sunshine might be the last chance. She didn't know whether to call it his or hers, let alone theirs.

In any case she was getting ready to lose him. Was he getting ready to lose her? She had no right to expect him to see it that way. Did she have any right to think she was losing him? She had never exactly had him. But oh yes she had.

She didn't know what it would be like to lose him, she didn't want to think about it, though lose him she must. Perhaps all she was thinking on the morning of Mothering Sunday, as she brought in more coffee at Beechwood, was that if he played his cards right with this day then she wanted him to play them with her. Some hope. Then the telephone had rung. "Wrong number." Her heart had soared.

"The shower will be leaving soon. I'll be on my tod here. Eleven o'clock. Front door."

He had spoken in a strong whisper, as if picturing her exact predicament, even down to the open breakfast-room door. It was an order, a curt order, but a transforming one. And she had listened, or appeared to listen, with polite patience, as if to some ineptly garrulous caller who had not yet realised their error.

"I'm awfully sorry, madam, but you have the wrong number."

How skilled she'd become, in seven years. At imitating their "awfully"s. And at other things too. But she still had to assimilate it: just the two of them in the empty house. It had never happened before. Front door. She had never been bidden to any front door. Though sometimes, in earlier days, it might have indicated his required form of congress.

"That's quite all right, madam."

Mr. Niven's munching on his toast and marmalade had perhaps obliterated some of her flawless performance.

"Wrong number," she'd explained. And then he'd given her half a crown.

And suppose he had known what things she'd once done for Paul Sheringham—to Paul Sheringham—yes, for only sixpence, sometimes for even less. And then, after not so long, for nothing, nothing at all, mutual interest in the transactions cancelling any need for purchase.

Though when she was eighty or ninety and

was asked, as she would be, even in public interviews, to look back on her younger years, she felt she could fairly claim (though of course never did) that one of her earliest situations in life was that of prostitute. Orphan, maid, prostitute.

HE TAPPED ASH into the ashtray decorating her belly.

AND SECRET LOVER. And secret friend. He had said that once to her, "You are my friend, Jay." He had said it so announcingly. It had made her head go light. She had never been called that, named that thing so decisively by anyone, as if he were saying he had no other friend, he had only just discovered, in fact, what a friend might be. And she was to tell no one about this newly attested revelation.

It had made her head swim. She was seventeen. She had ceased to be a prostitute. Friend. It was better perhaps than lover. Not that "lover" would have been then in her feasible vocabulary, or even in her thinking. But she would have lovers. In Oxford. She would have many of them, she would make a point of it. Though how many of them were friends?

And was Emma Hobday, even though she was his bride-to-be, his friend?

In any case, as friends or perhaps even as lovers, or just as young Mister Paul and the new Beechwood maid he'd spotted one day in the post office in Titherton, they'd done all sorts of things together, in all sorts of secret locations. The two houses were scarcely a mile apart, if you went by the back routes and then, necessarily, through the garden. The greenhouse and the disused part of the stables were just two of their recourses. And they'd done those things by a strangely depend-able intuition—you could hardly call it a time-table—that had become the habit, the telepathy of true friends. As if everything were always by imagined chance, but they knew it was not.

So—they were really lovers?

Because there was anyway such an intensity and strange gravity to their experimentation, such a consciousness at least that they were doing something wrong (the whole world was in mourning all around them), it had needed some compensating element of levity: giggling. It had sometimes seemed in fact that to get each other giggling was the real aim of it all—a dangerous aim to have when another essential factor was that they should on no account be found out.

And the remarkable thing was that even now, with his suave and superior ways and his silver cigarette case, there was a giggle still inside him, still there, even now when they'd become accomplished, unfumbling, serious-faced addicts at what they did. It might still suddenly emerge, without warning, without explanation, out of his polished exterior, an explosive cacophonous giggle, as if a mould had shattered.

But he was naked now, there was no mould to shatter. And why should he giggle? It was their last day.

SHE HAD SPED on her bicycle from Beechwood to Upleigh. That is, since Mr. and Mrs. Niven were yet to depart, she had been careful not to be seen to be hurrying at all, or to be pointing the bicycle in the direction of Upleigh. At the gate she had turned casually right not left. But then, after turning two more corners, she had sped.

Then, nearing Upleigh, she'd done something she had never done before. She had not approached by the usual back route, by the garden path—leaving her bicycle hidden in the familiar clump of hawthorns, then continuing, alertly, on foot. She had taken the front road and boldly cycled through the Upleigh gates and up the drive between the rows of lime trees and the swirls of daffodils.

It was what he had instructed—ordered her to do. The front door. It was only as she turned through the gates that the extraordinariness, the unprecedented gift of it—yes, it was *her* day— came to her. The front door! And he must have wanted to observe her do it, since hardly had she brought her bicycle to a halt near the porch than the front door—or rather one of them, there were two tall imposing glossy-black doors— opened, as if by a miraculous power of its own.

She did not know for certain, though she would soon, that his bedroom overlooked the drive. He might have been visible for a moment, had she been looking for him, at the open window on the first floor. But he was visible suddenly anyway, stepping from behind the apparently self-opening door—to be called "madam" by her, while she would be called "clever" by him. She'd propped the bicycle quickly against the front wall. The hall, beyond the vestibule, had black-and-white chessboard tiles. There were the fronds of intense white flowers.

"My mother's precious orchids. But we're not here to look at them."

And he'd led her—or rather steered her by her backside—up the stairs.

Then it might have been her turn to be called "madam," since, once inside the bedroom, he began almost immediately to undress her as he'd never done before—or rather as he'd never before had such an opportunity to do. Could it even strictly be said that he'd *ever* "undressed" her?

"Stand there, Jay. Stay still."

It seemed that he wanted her not to move, just to stand, while his fingers gradually undid and released everything and let it fall about her. So it was not at all unlike how she might sometimes, if Mrs. Niven should wearily request it, be required to "undo" Mrs. Niven. Except, she couldn't deny it, there was a reverence with which he went about the task that she could never have applied to Mrs. Niven. It was like an unveiling. She would never forget it.

"Don't move, Jay."

Meanwhile she could look around her at this remarkable room she had never been in before. A dressing table, with a triple-panelled mirror, cluttered with small objects, mainly silver. An armchair with a striped pattern, gold on cream. Curtains similarly patterned and completely drawn back (while he undressed her!) and gently stirring. An open window. A carpet of a pale grey-blue, the colour of cigarette smoke caught in sunlight—and sunlight was pouring in. A bed.

"What is this, Jay? Your hidden treasure?"

His fingers had found something in the recesses of her clothing.

A half-crown piece.

IT WAS Mothering Sunday 1924. Mr. Niven had indeed watched her unspeedily cycle off, since he'd just brought the Humber round to the front to await Mrs. Niven. She supposed that, most of the time, Mr. Niven would "undo" Mrs. Niven, if she couldn't undo herself. What a word—"undo"! She supposed that Mrs. Niven might now and then say, "Undo me, Godfrey," in a different way from how she might say it to her maid. Or that Mr. Niven might sometimes say in a different way still, "Can I undo you, Clarrie?"

She supposed that Mr. and Mrs. Niven might still, now and then ... even though some eight years ago they had lost two "brave boys." But she did not suppose. She occasionally saw the evidence. She changed the sheets.

She did not know, even on Mothering Sunday, what it would be like to be a mother and lose two sons—in as many months apparently. Or how such a mother might feel on such a day. No boys would be coming home, would they, with little posies or simnel cakes to offer?

But Paul Sheringham would be getting married in two weeks' time and he was the one son left. And of course the Nivens would be there. He was (and oh how he knew it) both families' darling.

NOW MR. AND MRS. NIVEN would be driving, sitting side by side, through the bright spring sunshine to Henley. Milly already, before any of them, had creaked her way out of the Beechwood gates to get the 10:20 from Titherton. And this house, Upleigh, was now obligingly empty, except for themselves, since Mr. and Mrs. Sheringham—"the shower"—had also departed for Henley, and the Upleigh cook and maid—Iris and Ethel—had been driven to Titherton Station by no less a person than Paul Sheringham.

Only now did he tell her this, as he undressed her—or rather, since she was soon standing naked in his sunlit room, as she, in reciprocal fashion, began to undress, to "undo," him.

"I drove Iris and Ethel to the station."

It was something that hardly needed announcing. Did it relate to what they were doing right now? And it was something—she thought later—that had hardly needed doing. On a morning like this Iris and Ethel might have been happy to walk. Upleigh was even closer to Titherton Station than Beechwood was.

Was it his way of explaining why his telephone call had come so agonisingly late? Or of assuring her that the house really was all safely theirs? He had packed off the staff himself.

But he had said it in such an untypically earnest way. As if he wished her to know, she would think later, that on this special upside-down day he had placed himself, lordliest of the lordly as he could be, in the deferring role. He had not only offered her his house, opened its door for her obediently on her arrival, then undressed her as if he were her slave, but he had, in this other way too, been of service to servants, kind to her kind.

"For the 9:40. I took them in the Ma-and-Pa-mobile."

Which would now perhaps be already parked somewhere in Henley. His own car, still in the stable-turned-garage, was a racy thing with a top that came down, only really meant for two.

Perhaps he did it every year, drove them to

the station. A Sheringham tradition. But then he said, "I wanted to give them a proper goodbye."

A proper goodbye? They might be back by teatime. They weren't going for ever.

Was it his roundabout way of saying that this was what he was giving *her*? A proper goodbye. She could hardly give it much thought at the time, since—his own clothes removed and quickly draped with hers over the armchair—they had moved, with no more ceremony, to the bed.

But she would think about it later. All her life she would picture it: the two women, awed and silent in the back of the big black saloon while he drove them, chauffeur-style. On the station forecourt he might have opened doors and helped them out with the same gracious atten-tiveness with which he'd removed her clothes. They might even have thought he was going to offer them each a kiss.

All her life she would try to see it, to bring back this Mothering Sunday, even as it receded and even as its very reason for existing became a historical oddity, the custom of another age. As he set them down the distant white puffs of the 9:40 to Reading might already have been visible in that brilliant blue sky. On the platform there might have been two or three others like Iris and Ethel waiting to set off on similar journeys (though not yet Cook Milly, who would get the 10:20).

All the maids. All the mothers getting out in readiness what passed for their best china. All the maids with their mothers to go to.

AND SHE KNEW the maid at Upleigh. She was called Ethel Bligh. Poor mouse. She had had conversations with Ethel—they met on errands at Sweeting's the grocer's in Titherton— conversations that scarcely became conversations and that never got near becoming gossip. The cook at Upleigh was a stout creature rather like Milly, but Ethel was a nimble-bodied maid, a little like herself. With another sort of Ethel she might not only have gossiped—the two of them leaning on their bicycles outside Sweeting's— but even giggled, even giggled just a tiny bit like she giggled with Paul Sheringham.

But even then she wouldn't have told this

other Ethel what she got up to with Mister Paul. Or rather this other Ethel would have known, guessed already. Or rather this other Ethel would have got in first, or have been got in first, being so handily under the same roof.

So it was just as well, in fact, that Ethel was not this other Ethel, but a good little maid who, without having to struggle much to do it, did what maids were constantly required to do: turned a blind eye and a deaf ear and, above all, kept a closed mouth.

Ethel might be going to her mother's today in the same spirit of meek submission with which she'd once offered her services to Mrs. Sheringham. The two things might have become indistinguishable.

Did she and Iris gossip? Surely they did. On the train after their tongue-tied car ride, did they suddenly start to talk? So what was all that about? Was it because he was getting married and would soon be—leaving them?

Or would they have sunk into deeper silence, unaccustomed as they were to being out in the world and to being reminded that they had lives, even mothers, of their own? Would they have just gawped and blinked at sun-bathed, lamb-dotted England?

While Paul Sheringham religiously undressed her.

"Stay still, Jay."

AND, EVEN AS he undressed her and as if to answer another, unspoken question of hers, he'd said, "I'm mugging up, Jay. My law books. That's what I'm doing now. Mugging up." It might have produced a giggle, from either of them, but it didn't. It was said with such an instructive urgency, as if, were she ever to be asked—interrogated—that's what she was to say that he, that they, had been doing.

It would pass into her private unconfessable code-language, standing for so much that was beyond telling anyway. She would never be able to hear the phrase lightly, even in Oxford, where a great deal of mugging up went on.

But it had been his ruse for getting out of the Henley expedition and for securing the house for himself—and her. It was also, neatly, like a virtuous pledging of his future responsibilities. When they were married he and Emma Hobday were going to live in London (this she knew and could only bleakly accept) and he was supposed to be going to make an honest man out of himself and even an honest living—regardless of his new access to "loot"—by studying to become a lawyer.

How times, indeed, could change.

So even today, even on such a glorious morning, he would demonstrate his commitment to this plan with a spot of serious mugging up. It was unlike him, it was out of character, but hardly to be objected to. Perhaps there being only two weeks left—so they might be chucklingly surmising in Henley—had brought out this sudden rush of conscientiousness in him.

Except that he knew and she knew—did Miss Hobday know?—that he had about as much intention of becoming a lawyer as becoming a lettuce.

"We're mugging up, Jay." If anyone should ask.

Though it still left one unanswered, and not even asked, question. She didn't dare ask it, or want to ask it. It was for him to say.

Assuming that he (they) would not be—

mugging up—all day, what other separate arrangement might there be, might he have in place, with Miss Hobday?

THEY LAY side by side, uncovered, flicking ash, not talking, watching the smoke from their cigarettes rise up and merge under the ceiling. For a while such smoke-sharing was enough. She thought of the white puffs from trains. Their cigarettes, now and then merely lodged vertically in their lips, were like miniature companion chimneys.

There was only the bird-chatter outside and the strangely audible, breath-held silence of the empty house, and the faint ripple of air over their bodies, reminding them, though they eyed the ceiling, that they were entirely naked. Two fish on a white plate, she thought. Two pink salmon on a sideboard, waiting for guests, guests at a wedding even, who would never arrive . . .

She did not want to say, to ask, anything that might puncture the possibility of their staying like this for ever.

It was called "relaxation," she thought, a word that did not commonly enter a maid's vocabulary. She had many words, by now, that did not enter a maid's vocabulary. Even the word "vocabulary." She gathered them up like one of those nest-building birds outside. And was she even a maid any more, stretched here on his bed? And was he even a "master"? It was the magic, the perfect politics of nakedness.

More than relaxation: peace.

With one hand, the other holding her cigarette, she just brushed, not looking, his moist cock, feeling it stir almost instantly, like some sleeping nestling. As if she might have done such a thing all her life, an idle duchess, stroking a puppy. Only moments ago, with the same hand twisted back to grasp one of the brass rods of the bedstead—this bed she'd never been in before— she'd pressed with the other hand, palm flat but fingers digging, the small of his back, pressed hard the place where it seemed his cock joined his spine. She was commanding him—what command could be stronger and more bidding? Yet he had commanded her: the front door.

Now it seemed that what they'd just done was only a doorway itself to this supreme region of utter mutual nakedness.

Peace. It was true of all days, it was the trite truth of any day, but it was truer today than on any day: there never was a day like this, nor ever would or could be again.

HER CIGARETTE WAS burning down. She moved the little ashtray—it was surely her prerogative—onto the strip of sheet between them. It was her belly, she might have said, it wasn't a table, she didn't want him stubbing his cigarette out against it—much as she might actually have liked it. And how she would remember that ashtray coolly resting on her belly.

Then she wished she hadn't been so fastidious or presumptuous, hadn't done anything at all.

He took the cigarette from his mouth and simply held it, upright, against his own belly.

"I have to meet her at half past one. At the Swan Hotel at Bollingford."

He didn't otherwise move, but it was like

the breaking of a spell. And only anyway what she must have anticipated. Though she thought she might have passed, by magic dispensation, beyond that "must." The rest of the day? One portion of it couldn't (could it?) last for ever. One fragment of a life cannot be the all of it.

She didn't stir, but she might have, inwardly, altered. As if she might have had her clothes invisibly on again, might even be turning back into a maid.

But nor did he stir, as if in his stillness countering—belying—what he'd just said. He didn't have to keep his appointment, did he? Who said so? He didn't have to do a damn thing he didn't want to, did he? He might simply lie here and ignore it.

And "her"—not "Emma." It was like some dismissal shared between them. And "I have to."

His cigarette was almost finished.

He didn't move, nor did she, as if in fact he hadn't just spoken. Yet equally as if the slightest movement on her part, let alone a sound, a word, might have been to acknowledge that he'd said it and so commit him to its consequences.

It was not her place, after all, with her ghostly maid's clothes back on again, to speak, suggest or do more than wait. Years of training had conditioned her. They are creatures of mood and whim. They might be nice to you one moment, but then— And if they snapped or barked, you must jump. Or rather take it in your stride, carry on, not seethe. Yes sir, yes madam. And always—it was half the trick—be ready for it.

Then it came to her that the whole thing might be turned the other way round. This upside-down day. She was lying here with him in his room, like his wife, and he was brazenly consulting with her as to whether he should go and see his troublesome mistress. Some couples, some of their kind, might actually do this. And wasn't it in fact, at heart, like that? He wasn't yet married. To either of them. She and Emma Hobday were equals.

He did not speak, as if enough silence after his remark, for all its apparent call for punctuality, might cancel everything. And he was perfectly capable of such contempt for nicety. Of having it both ways. He hadn't been dishonest, had he? He just hadn't acted accordingly. It was his way: he misbehaved, but he didn't lie about it.

And he'd taken Ethel and Iris nobly to the station.

And she wasn't going to say, like some remarkably forbearing wife, "Then you'd better go, hadn't you?" Was he really asking her to?

His lengthening silence might have given her an increasing power—or compliance. But the moment was passing when he might have said, "But I think we have the whole day, Jay, don't you?" Putting his hand where the ashtray had been. Or a little lower.

It must happen. He would go to her and have his lunch with her and even perhaps, somehow or other, later today, have his entitled way with her. If that is how it was between them. He might even bring her back here to do so. To this very room. She hadn't asked him when his "shower" were expected to return. He was in charge of that contingency. They would hardly yet have sat down to lunch in Henley.

And now, with his own lunch plans sud-denly hovering in the air, but with their clothes still strewn together over the armchair, their moment already was passing. He didn't have that much time.

Moment? It was too mean a word. Hour? Day? Gift? But it was slipping away, as the day had already slipped away from the peak of noon. He must have looked at the little clock, or at his silver pocket watch, on the dressing table when he got up to fetch the cigarettes.

And there was the unalterable truth that it might never have happened at all. And, yes, she should be grateful, eternally grateful. "I wanted to give them a proper goodbye." She might have been touring Berkshire on a bicycle.

And he might, by the same connivance, have brought "her" here anyway. His telephone call might have been to the Hobday residence. "She" might have had to speak into the telephone just as slyly and pretendingly. Did they communicate in such ways? Then turned up here, crunching the gravel, in her car. The Emmamobile. She might be here with him *now*.

But she couldn't imagine it. Her flowery dress over the chair, her silky underwear. She was the one actually lying here, and shouldn't she be grateful? Even if he'd be lying here beside the other one later. Two in one day. Was it possible? The Swan at half past one. But she couldn't imagine it.

At the back of her mind was the scrambling thought that if his wife-to-be was in some way "arranged" then the arrangement might include that she must be a flawless, untouched virgin, as if he were marrying a vase. And unlikely as it was—that *he* could promise himself to a vase—there must be some truth in her thought or some other reason for his lack of soon-to-be-married enthusiasm. If it were not the plain fact that he was lying here now with her.

IN ANY CASE after minutes of mere stillness, of almost defiant inertia, he suddenly moved, and with an excessive upheaval of his limbs. The whole mattress rocked like a boat. He picked up the slipping ashtray and crushed the stub of his cigarette brutally against it.

And it was then, as she lifted one knee to

counter the commotion, that she felt the trickle from between her legs: his seed leaving her, along with liquid of her own. She had other words than "seed," but she liked the word "seed." It might have happened at any moment, but its happening now, along with its seeping sadness, seemed almost like a sudden riposte. Well, it would be difficult for him now to be here, later, with her, the flowery one, if that was part of his plan.

Unless he were to tell her right now—she was still a maid, if not his—to replace the sheets.

It was crude arguing. It was what animals, who made no marriage vows and kept no servants, relied on. They marked their territory.

And she wasn't going to say, now he was on his feet and the decision all but made, "Please, don't go. Please, don't leave me." She was disqualified from the upper world in which such dramas were staged. She had her lowly contempt for such stuff anyway. As if she couldn't have used—but she wasn't his wife, it was all the other way round—a different, quieter but fiercer language. Or just the bullet of a look.

In any case, there was the trickle between her legs.

He moved across the room. He might be going only to consult the time. Once again she was able to view him in his surly nakedness. Yes, he had a different walk without his clothes on, an animal walk.

He turned at the dressing table to look at her, holding his watch now in his hand. She hadn't moved, dared to move, herself. There was only her lifted, theoretically coaxing knee, only her own unhiding nakedness to make him think again. He was taking it in, no more abashed, once again, about his looking than about his own display of himself. His cock was a little fuller but still merely hanging. And now he was familiarly winding the watch, blindly dealing with it even as he gazed.

"Not quite a quarter to. If I step on it, I should make it. We're meeting halfway. The Swan. She knows the people there. It was her idea."

As if she, the Beechwood maid, knew anything about the Swan Hotel at Bollingford or how long it took to get there by car. But the party at Henley would have known? The young things were having their own private lunch. Well, you couldn't blame them. After he'd commendably spent the morning with his law books.

But there was the little matter now of his getting dressed, of his making himself presentable, of his putting together again his outward person. He seemed in no hurry to do so. He looked at her, his eyes ran up and down her. He must have surely noticed the little patch between her legs.

She'd never known him show, even when actually hurrying, any sense of haste or unseemly agitation. Except, that is—but it seemed suddenly a very long time ago—when it had all been a boy's uncurbable rush. She'd sometimes said to him, "Slow down." She'd even said, as if she were steeped in experience herself, "Slower is better."

Well, they were steeped in experience now. He had never known anyone better, she was sure of it. Nor had she. It was in the look he gave her now. And in the stare she returned.

She found it difficult, even as she stared, not to let tears come into her eyes, even as she knew that to allow them, use them, would have been somehow to fail. She must be brave, generous, merciless in allowing him this last possible gift of herself.

Would he ever forget her, lying there like that?

And he *was* in no hurry. The sun from the window lit him. A bar or two of shadow ran across his torso. He finished winding the watch. His eventual car journey must be getting impossibly fast.

She didn't know how he had acquired his sureness. Later, in her memory, she would marvel at it and be almost frightened by his possession of it then. It was the due of his kind? He was born to it. It came with having no other particular thing to do? Except be sure. But that, surely, would flood you with unsureness. On the other hand, to be a lawyer, merely a lawyer—she even felt it for him and saw him in a lawyer's imprisoning dark suit—could only take his sureness away.

She thought momentarily and madly: Supposing she—Emma, Miss Hobday—had come to get him anyway. Supposing—this was 1924, it

was the modern age—she had taken it upon herself to come here, in her car, to collect him now.
To surprise him, drag him from his "mugging
up." On such a marvellous day. Wheels on the
gravel. Her flowery voice—with a slight touch
of horse—shouting up, as she noticed the opened
window, knowing that it was his bedroom.

"Come to get you, Paul! Where are you?"

What then? She had no doubt that he would
have handled it all, somehow, surely. Even wearing just his signet ring. Even standing at the
window. "Emsie, darling! What a surprise! Give
me a mo to put a shirt on, would you?"

And how might she, the Nivens' maid in the
Sheringhams' house, have handled it?

On the dressing table beside him were all the
other little accoutrements of his life, sentimen-
tal or purposeful, each one like his own piece
of unhidden treasure. Hairbrushes and combs.
Cufflinks and studs in boxes. Photos in silver
frames. A preponderance of silver, kept bright
by Ethel. Maids had perpetually to dust round,
not to mention actually polish, such parapher-
nalia, making sure nothing was moved from

its ordained position. Well, it was easier than a woman's dressing table.

If you were brought up with such stuff attached to you, such personal insignia, then perhaps it was easy to be sure. Not to mention the contents of his wardrobe, in the adjacent dressing room—she had briefly seen it as she was bustled in. All his hanging choices. Not to mention other possessions scattered round the house.

All that she owned or wore could be put in one plain box. If she had to leave in a hurry, and she always might, she could.

But it was these little trinkets, this boys' jewellery that seemed now to claim him, confirm him. Signet ring. Pocket watch. Cufflinks. When he was dressed and before he left he would gather up the initialled cigarette case and lighter. He would run the hairbrush across his hair, apply the tortoiseshell comb. His two brothers must have taken an assortment of such things, much of it perhaps newly and morale-boostingly purchased, when they went across to France, never to come back. Ivory-handled shaving brushes, that sort of thing. They, the brothers, were on the dressing table now, in silver frames. She'd noticed them as soon as she entered the room. That must be Dick and Freddy. Both in officers' caps. She'd never seen them before. How could she have?

She'd looked at them as he'd undone her clothes.

HE PADDED OUT of the room to the bathroom. Still only the signet ring. He wasn't there for long. He had only to wash and rinse himself, whatever men did. Remove, that is, all imme-diate traces of herself on him. She would think about this later.

The room seemed to close in on her during his short absence, even to claim her as part of its furniture. She did not move. She lay indeed like an inanimate object, though she was all tingling flesh. He had made no sign to her that she *should* move—that now he'd got up, it might be proper for her to do the same. Rather the opposite. It was no surprise to him, when he reappeared, that she was still tenaciously lying there. It was what, it seemed, he had even expected, wanted her to do.

He had a scent about him now that she might have appreciated, save that it cancelled out the sweeter smell of his sweat. She would think about this too later: that he put on his cologne. But he was still naked and in no apparent haste. He had brought in, from the dressing room, a fresh white shirt, a pale-grey waistcoat and a tie, but it seemed that the rest of his outfit would consist of what he'd discarded on the chair. He might have done all his dressing in the dressing room, but perhaps this was his habit anyway, to dress by the light of the window, by his dressing table and its angled mirrors. The dressing room was merely a wardrobe.

But it seemed that he did not want to be separated from her, though he was about to leave. It was in some way all for her—that she should watch him dress, watch his nakedness gradually disappear. Or that he just didn't care. The sureness, the aloofness, the unaccountable unhurriedness. She should leave too? But he said nothing and she remained, as if now actually commanded to, where she was, while his eyes travelled over her again, even as he dressed.

He must have noticed the trickle. But it was part of his fine disdain not to notice it. It was like the clothes he might leave pooled on the floor, to find their way back to him, laundered and pressed, hanging in the dressing room. These were things to be cleared up discreetly by people who cleared up such things. And she, normally, was such a one. She was part of the magic army that permitted such disregard. Was he really going to tell her, before he left, to deal with the mess? And give her her cheap moment to remind him that she was not his servant?

But she saw as he looked at her—and surely at that incriminating patch—that such a squalid little scene was far from his thoughts. Some other kind of indifference was making him careless of such a minor matter as a stain on a sheet. Was it a stain, anyway, that it should be removed? Any more than she should remove herself—and she was not a stain—from his bed. Yes, he *wanted* her to be there, when it might have been her role, in another life, in a commoner, comic story, to be already scurrying downstairs, still adjusting her clothing. It was his wish, before he left, to see her there, to have her there, nakedly and—who knows?—immovably occupying his bedroom, so that the image of her would be there, branding itself on his mind, even as he met—his vase.

She was doing, as she lay there, the right, the finest thing. She understood it, even as she understood that her lying there had lost all argument, all pleading for his not going. He was clearly going. And he wanted her, for some reason she couldn't fathom, to watch, even as she blazoned her nakedness, this business of his getting dressed, of his putting back on again the life that was his.

Why was he being so slow?

The room had been filled now with as much light and unseasonal warmth as was possible. The minute hand on his watch must be moving towards one, even beyond it. The dark line on the sundial in the garden at Beechwood—where she might have been sitting right now, a book on her lap—would have crept further round. She could not make out the face of the little clock on the dressing table—the two brothers, either side, guarding it.

Was there ever such a day as this? Could there ever be such a day again?

IT WOULD BE Ethel's job, she realised, to deal with the stain—the trickle, the patch. Ethel who would even now, she imagined, be sitting in a house filled with the pricey smell of roasting beef—on such a warm day, when a bit of cold ham might have served. Sitting where her mother had commanded her to sit and not get up or lift a finger. It was her day off, wasn't it? Today everything was different, special. "Talk to your dad for a while, Ethel." If Ethel still had a dad, or a dad still in one piece. For these few hours of reunion, of mother-honouring, Ethel's mother would toil in the kitchen and Ethel's mother and father would live for a week on bread and dripping.

But Ethel when she returned to her duties later—when "the shower" would have perhaps also returned, invigorated yet fatigued from

their sunny outing and in need of attention—
would have to change the sheets in Mister Paul's
bedroom, not having been present earlier to do
so, and would notice the stain. In so far as Ethel
noticed such things, since it was her job simul-
taneously to notice them and quickly make it
seem that they had never existed.

Even Ethel, who had sat down only hours ago,
like royalty, to roast meat, would know what
such a stain was. It was the common lot of her
kind to come upon them, in bedrooms. So much
so that they were sometimes known, in below-
stairs parlance, as "come-upons." There were
other expressions, of varying inventiveness,
including "maps of the British Isles." If there
had to be any actual, awkward professional dis-
cussion of them, they might be officially known
as "nocturnal emissions"—which did not necessarily cover all circumstances and might not
leave a new maid of sixteen fully enlightened.
Little boys—not so little boys—had nocturnal
emissions that, setting aside the fact that they
might have had them more considerately, had to
be rendered rapidly absent.

All this she had gleaned for herself before

arriving at Beechwood, when she had been briefly dispatched, as part of her "training" and on a sort of probation, to a big house requiring extra staff for the summer occupancy. There had been five maids in all and, my, how some of them had talked.

There were many emissions that were not produced solitarily and were not, directly, emissions at all (or even necessarily nocturnal), and most maids, using their powers of deduction, could tell the difference and, using their powers of deduction further, might even draw conclusions as to exactly how the "emission" had been formed. But this was not in any way to be spoken of or even acknowledged. Though it was one of the things that could make a maid's work interesting. All the stains, all the permutations. A summer house party with twenty-four guests. Oh Lord.

And even Ethel would have her deductions and conclusions, though she would be staunch in pretending she'd never had to have them. And Ethel's conclusion would be that in the period of time in which the house would have been (supposedly) vacated, Mister Paul would have taken the opportunity to entertain his fiancée, Miss Hobday, in his bedroom. For no other reason, possibly, than that they could do such a thing and get away with it. Setting aside that they might have waited. In two weeks' time they would not need to be such pranksters. Setting aside what kind of woman (one did not discuss Mister Paul) it suggested Miss Hobday was.

It was not for her, Ethel, to judge. Further deduction, along with received, whispered knowledge, might have told Ethel that Miss Hobday was at least one kind of woman: Mister Paul had not invited her to Upleigh for the express purpose of deflowering her. But in any case Ethel, already gathering up the sheets for the laundry basket, would assume that Mister Paul, if he'd taken stock of the stain at all, would have known that she, Ethel, would make it vanish, like the good fairy she was.

Except, as it would turn out, the whole situation—the whole atmosphere and needs of the household—would be different. No one, certainly, would be interested, if they ever had been, in whether Ethel had had a good time with her mother. And anyway Ethel would already have changed the sheets.

SHE HAD NEVER watched a man get dressed before. Though she had to deal intimately with men's garments, and during that summer at the big house had been rapidly educated in the astonishing range of them that one man might own and in their complications and intricacies. Though she had often and in a strange variety of places (stables, greenhouse, potting shed, shrubbery) interfered intimately with Paul Sheringham's clothes, even as he was wearing them, on the condition of course—or, rather, assumption—that he could interfere with hers.

He put the shirt on first, the clean white shirt he'd brought from the dressing room. To put it on—or, rather, enter it—he hoisted it above his head, like any woman tunnelling into a shift. She hadn't thought it would be the shirt first. But to every act of gentlemanly dressing there must be a mix of personal preference and prescribed order. In the "old days," after all, a manservant might have "dressed" him. Just as she could still be required to "dress" as well as "undo" Mrs. Niven.

Dressing, anyway, among their kind, was never conceived of as just a flinging on of clothes. It was a solemn piecing together. Though, in the circumstances, he had every reason to be flinging his clothes on as fast as he could. Another man, in another story, might be saying, as he madly tugged and tucked, "Christ, Jay, I have to damn well scoot!"

But his shirt first. That surprised her. Since it meant an immediate loss of dignity, the very thing that in his absence of haste he seemed bent on preserving. It was his trick, she would later think, it was always Paul Sheringham's great trick, to have such scorn for indignity that he never actually underwent it. He had lost his dignity and found it again so many times with her. But any man in just his shirt became automatically comic, and had it been some other story she might well have giggled.

She supposed that there must be two essential choices: the shirt to be tucked into the waiting trousers, or the trousers to receive the waiting

shirt. Each might have its advantages. Yet he
looked for a moment like a clown or, instead
of a man about to face the world (and a fum-
ing fiancée), like an overgrown boy made ready
for bed.

Once it would have been so, she thought. A
boy in a nightshirt. Once, he had told her—
a rare door opening to the past—about Nanny
Becky, who'd left when he'd been sent to school.
Once, he would have had a nanny to dress and
undress him, all three brothers would have
had her.

And what a strange thing, a nanny, a substitute mother. Presenting the offspring to their
parents at five o'clock, like a cook offering a cake.
And where was Nanny Becky now? In some
other household presumably. Or at her mother's.

SHE DID NOT giggle at his shirt. It might have
been nice to giggle, from her vantage point on
the bed. There might have been another world,
another life in which all this might have been a
regular, casual repertoire. But there wasn't. She

might have been some lounging wife in a room in London, watching him dress to be a joke of a lawyer.

They had hardly spoken for some time. A little while ago they'd made gasping, groaning animal noises. It seemed that they'd entered some diminishing gap of existence together in which, to use a phrase only to be known to her in later life, only "body language" might apply. Only her body might speak. She did not want to falsify—or nullify—anything by the folly of putting it into words. And this, in her later life too, would come to be an abiding occupational conundrum.

It seemed that any words they spoke now must be only ruinous banalities. Even as he engaged with the banalities of underpants and socks.

Yet he was putting on his finery. The fresh white shirt. It was a formal shirt. It would require a collar. It was not just a clean soft-collared shirt that might serve for a Sunday outing, a spin in a car with the top down. It was—even then in a rather old-fashioned sense—his "Sunday best."

She watched while he dealt, with unflustered skill, with cufflinks—little silver ovals winking in the sunshine—with collar studs and collar, semi-stiff. He had brought in a tie, a restrained but sheeny thing of slate blue with little white spots. He selected a tie pin. Was that actually, really a tiny diamond? His chin was already smooth—she'd had occasion to feel it—and now anointed with cologne.

It was as if he was dressing for his wedding. But it was not his wedding—yet. He was only going to meet his wife-to-be for a lunch by the River Thames. And if, as now seemed almost certain, he was going to be seriously late, how on earth was being so superbly turned-out going to help?

He had tied his tie studiously, giving due attention to the knot and the hanging lengths before fixing the pin, and all of this still without his trousers on. She did not, could not laugh. Yet it would seem to her later that everything had hinged upon this piece of farcical theatre. Once he put on his trousers all would be lost. If only she had said to him, screamed at him, "Don't put them on!"

But he went now again to the dressing room, lingering there (did he think time had stopped?) for several rustling minutes, then returned, with trousers on, as well as a jacket and shoes, even with a silk handkerchief, exactly complementing his tie, poking from his pocket.

So had it all been because he hadn't decided yet on the trousers—the ones he'd earlier discarded or ones still hanging in the dressing room? She would never know. She would never say, or be able to say, so he could make some quip or elucidate it all, "You took a long time putting on your trousers."

"Ah yes, Jay. So I did."

What a preposterous word anyway: "trousers."

HE STOOD THERE, complete. He gathered the cigarette case and lighter. He needed only, perhaps, a buttonhole. There were the white orchids in the hall. He might actually have been leaving for his wedding. It wasn't today, but he was signalling it anyway, it was perhaps what all this elaborate sprucing was about: he was leaving— wasn't he?—for his marriage. She felt an actual sting of jealousy for the woman who would be the recipient of all this dawdling decking-out. If she wasn't already in a fury of affrontedness.

And *she*, lying here, had had his unwrapped nakedness.

Then it struck her that it might all in fact have been simply for *her. Her* last look. His "going-away" clothes. Surely not. All the same, in spite of herself—they were the first words she'd spoken for some time—she said, "You look very handsome." She tried to make it sound not like some maid's blushing and inappropriate cooing—"Ooo you do look 'andsome, sir"—nor, on the other hand, like some royal approval. "You pass muster, you may go now." She tried to make it not sound even like the steady veiled declaration she wanted it to be.

He did not say to her, "And you look beautiful." He had never said that, never used that word. Only the word "friend." She couldn't even be sure there wasn't some shadow of discomfort in his face at the tribute she'd just paid him.

Only banality would do. Demolish—but do. He delivered a whole speech of it now.

"You don't have to hurry. I don't suppose the

shower will be back till at least four. When you go, lock the front door and put the key under the rock by the boot-scraper. It's not a rock, actually, it's half a stone pineapple. From when Freddy took a swing at it with his cricket bat. But it's what we do, whenever we leave the house empty. Which is hardly ever. And I'm not leaving it empty now, am I? But the shower will expect it—with no Ethel or Iris—if they get back first. It's a whacking great key, they won't have taken it themselves. I'll put it on the hall table. That's all really. Leave everything."

Did he mean by that the sheets, his shirt, his rejected trousers, dangling over the chair? What else could he mean? Was he telling her not to be a bloody maid? All this while he fingered the knot of his tie and tweaked at his cuffs.

"If you're hungry, there's a veal-and-ham pie, or half of one, in the kitchen. I can always tell Cookie I scoffed it. I mean—as well as going out to lunch. Not that I have to tell anyone anything. Anything."

It was his last, oddly echoing remark. Was it just about the veal-and-ham pie?

And later she would chew over not just a

veal-and-ham pie but almost every word of that matter-of-fact speech. It would stay eerily imprinted. But, precisely because of that, it would sometimes seem that she had made it up, that he could not have said all those things that she remembered so clearly, even fifty years later. He might have just said after all, "You'd better get some clothes on, you'd better make yourself scarce."

She would brood over it like some passage that perhaps needed redrafting, that might not yet have arrived at its proper meaning.

Then he was gone. No goodbye. No silly kiss. Just one last look. Like a draining of her, like a drinking up. And what he'd just bestowed on her: his whole house. He was leaving it to her. It was hers, for her amusement. She might ransack it if she wished. All hers. And what was a maid to do with her time, released for the day on Mothering Sunday, when she had no home to go to?

SHE LISTENED to his steps receding down the staircase. They became louder again as they clicked and loitered on the tiles of the hall. He was gathering an item or two before his actual departure? A hat? The buttonhole? Why not? Perhaps he kept a pin for such a thing in his jacket pocket. He was finding that key?

She did not move. She froze. She heard the front door—or doors—being opened, then closed. It was neither a slam nor a gentle manipulation. Then she heard—it came up from outside through the open window, not echoing through the house itself—his sudden giggle. If giggle it was. It was more like some trumpeting, defiant call, weird and startling as a peacock's. She would never forget it.

There was the crunch of his shoes on the gravel. He was walking towards the old stable and his garaged car. He would see her bicycle against the front wall. She'd simply propped it there, since he'd said the front door—and the front door had already been opening magically. She hadn't left it discreetly out of sight. And so, she realised now, if Miss Hobday had decided to turn up mischievously, as a fiancée might in this modern age, in her own car, to surprise him—and surprise him she would have done—she would have seen it: a woman's bicycle, without a crossbar. And then there might have been a scene, a wild and frantic scene. And the day would have turned out very differently.

But wasn't there going to be a scene now in any case, at the Swan at Bollingford?

All the scenes. All the scenes that never occur, but wait in the wings of possibility. It was perhaps already almost half past one. Birds chorused. Somewhere on a road the other side of Bollingford, Emma Hobday, in her Emmamobile, would already be nearing the place of their rendezvous. Or perhaps she too was late. It was her woman's right. Perhaps she was always maddeningly late and perhaps he was only banking on this exasperating habit. If he timed it right they might serenely coincide.

Perhaps that was the simple explanation.

But in any case Emma Hobday would be enjoying, as she drove, the dazzling rush of this spring day. What it might be like to drive a car was beyond her maid's experience—she had only driven a bicycle. But she tried to put herself momentarily in the shoes—or on the wheels—of Emma Hobday who did not know yet what a show of himself her husband-to-be had prepared for her. Or that he'd taken so long in putting on his trousers.

And at Henley they might have finished the smoked salmon and be anticipating perhaps the duck or the lamb with mint sauce—surely not as good as Milly's. And remarking yet again on the marvellous weather, and if only it would repeat itself for the wedding. She imagined a dining room with tall French windows flung open to the sunshine. A lawn leading down to the river. Tables even, laid up, outside. White hats. Like a wedding itself.

All the scenes. To imagine them was only to imagine the possible, even to predict the actual. But it was also to conjure the non-existent.

She heard the car start. A throaty revving or two. Perhaps he always did it, as if a race was starting. And he would surely have to race now, to redeem himself even partially. But she heard the wheels simply crackle, not spin or lurch, over the gravel, then the sound of the engine gathering speed and noise, as he drove between the lime trees and the two big lawns, then getting fainter and simply merging with the birdsong.

She did not move. She did not go to the window. A brief, flourishing roar, as he turned onto the metalled road—the same road he had taken this morning, in the other car, with the honoured but cowed Ethel and Iris—and at last put his foot down.

She didn't move. The curtains stirred slightly. A naked girl in his room. She didn't move—she didn't know how long she didn't move—until it seemed the absurdity of her not moving won out against some dreadful need not to.

Then she moved. She reared up from the pillow. Her feet found the carpet. She walked over it, naked, as he had. The two brothers in their silver frames stared at her. She saw herself in the mirror. She went to the window. There was nothing to see. Berkshire. There was no one to notice her sudden unaccountable face at the window, her bare sunlit breasts. The sky was an unbroken blue.

She turned back into the room, resisting the fleeting urge to begin picking up clothes. She looked at the bed where they had both been, the covers flung back, the dented sheets, the little blatant stain.

She thought of Ethel.

All the emissions. Ethel, maid in a house of boys, would be not unfamiliar with them, though this little stain would be curiously different. All the emissions of three brothers, and two of them gone now. Though there they were, in their silver frames, eyeing a naked girl. And Ethel, she strongly supposed, had never known what it was like to be the direct cause of a man's emission, let alone to feel it inside her, or, mingling with her own fluids, trickling out of her. A maid—and, yes, a maid. And Ethel must be nearing thirty. Her parents must be ancient. But at least she had them and had been allowed to see them today.

All the wasted emissions. The sunlight for a moment seemed to be filling the room only with a bright bare emptiness. But why should she be feeling so bereft and alone in the world when she'd had what she'd had this day? And when, after all, she wasn't Ethel. And when she had right now a whole house along with a small parkland at her disposal—as Mr. Niven might have put it.

SHE WALKED OUT, past the dressing room, into the nearby bathroom. A little masculine temple. She looked at razors and brushes and bottles of cologne and wondered whether to touch them. She wondered whether to touch and finger every last item on the glass shelves. She washed and dried herself anyway, using the basin and the towel—damp from his own use of it—that Ethel would remove unthinkingly.

She'd put in the cap that he'd helped her get. It was why there had been so much dribble. She couldn't have got such a thing without him, and it had all been done, with his usual scorning of difficulty or embarrassment, one day when she'd had the afternoon off. She'd got the 1:20 to Reading and met him. Afterwards, they'd gone to a cinema.

God knows how he'd arranged it. He out-clevered her, perhaps, at some things. "There's a doctor chappie I know, Jay . . ." It had taken her some time to—adapt to it. It was her (their) precious means of prevention.

And suppose, she would think later, she *had* become pregnant. Would she have suffered all the consequences—they would have been all *her* consequences and would have included swift banishment—so that his marriage would not have been cancelled? Would she have borne all that for him?

Suppose she had deliberately neglected to put the thing in, say three months ago.

Suppose.

"A Dutch cap, Jay. So my seed doesn't get anywhere near you. I mean, any nearer than it needs to."

She didn't know what was Dutch about it. But part of her maid's outfit was a little white cap. So there were times when she was wearing two caps.

And "seed." That was another strange word, or it was a strange way of using it, since it didn't look like anything resembling seed—the pips in an apple, the tiny black things that might dust a loaf. And yet it was the proper and the right word, she could see that too, and she rather liked it. And it was the word he'd first used for it, when she first became acquainted with the stuff. "It's my seed, Jay." It seemed so long ago now. "It's my seed. We could put it in the ground and water it and see what happens." She honestly hadn't known if he was being serious.

And now it was springtime. Seed time. "We plough the fields and scatter . . ."

All the emissions.

Had her mother been a pregnant maid? Was that the whole story? Had her mother not had a cap to put in? All the omissions. As Milly might have put it.

SHE WENT INTO the dressing room. She was tempted to touch, finger—even try on—every-thing that hung in it. It was something that servants could only wonder at. What will it be today? Who shall I be today? How had he chosen, on such a day, his almost severe yet perfect steel-grey jacket?

She went back into the bedroom. There was the soft onslaught of the birdsong again. The far-off snorting of a train.

She might retrieve her clothes, put them on and leave at once. What was the phrase she had sometimes read in books? "Cover her tracks." But he'd said what he'd said: the house was hers. She would truly make it so. And it would have seemed somehow like a wrongness, a retreat, to put her clothes back on again.

She went out onto the landing, into shadow, her bare feet on mossy carpet. Shafts and dapples of sunlight from some upper window or skylight caught the red and brown weaves beneath her, the worn patch at the top of the staircase, the gleam of banisters, the glitter of dust in the air. There was always dust in the air. Why else the need for dusting?

She descended the stairs, her fingers stroking the rail more out of delicate assessment than to steady herself. Where the stairs turned, stair rods gleamed. Ethel was no slouch. Below, the hall seemed to tense at her approach. Objects might have scuttled and retreated. They had never witnessed anything like this before. A naked woman coming down the stairs!

Her feet struck the coolness of the hall tiles. On one side of the exit to the vestibule was a grandfather clock, on the other a full-length mirror. Across the hall was a table with the large bowl and the sprigs of white flowers. His mother's precious orchids. They did not look like any other flower. They had a stillness, an insistence, each little bloom was like a frozen butterfly.

Might he have picked one before he left? They looked indeed too precious to be picked. But what should he care? It was not his way to respect such things. As it was not his way, plainly, to respect punctuality. The grandfather clock said a quarter to two! And who would notice one little flower missing from the stem? If there was one missing now, she wasn't noticing it.

It was all in her head, in any case, that he might have picked an orchid. Then stood before the mirror to attach it. As was the picture that she might have stood here and picked one for him. "Here—before you go." And held it to his lapel.

Pictures hung around the hall, as they hung, in step-fashion themselves, above the stairs, as they hung also around the walls at Beechwood. It was a strange thing, this need among their kind for pictures to adorn the walls, since she had never seen Mr. or Mrs. Niven actually stand before a picture and look at it. They were things, perhaps, only to be noted out of the corner of the eye, or only for visitors to appreciate. Or rather for maids to study closely and be their true connoisseurs, as they dusted the frames and cleaned the glass.

She had stared repeatedly at all the pictures at Beechwood, so that she would remember them always, even when she was ninety, like some thumbed catalogue in her head, as people apparently remembered with uncanny clarity the illustrations in their first children's books. As she would remember always the big gloomy pictures of men in dark coats—benefactors, overseers—that hung in the hall in the orphanage, where there had been no reading of bedtime stories.

Could she "catalogue" this place? Or at least

take in and preserve in some way its sudden crowding presence for her, its multiplicity of contents. Given that she would never be here again. Given that she could only give it so long—how long might she dare?

And how long before, for him, the catalogue of this place, in his new life, might seep from his head? Not quickly, she imagined, even hoped. And how long before, for him, the catalogue of all the moments with her . . . ? Before even this day would fade.

WITHIN THE VESTIBULE—it was much like at Beechwood—there were all the regular accompaniments—umbrella stand, hat stand—of departures and arrivals, gatherings or sheddings of coats. Here (though it was Ethel's task) she might easily have stood to practise that essential art of the servant of being both invisible yet indispensably at hand. She was invisible now.

On a little felt-topped narrow table where gloves and other belongings might sometimes rest she saw the key that he'd left out for her. It was large and very key-like and somehow like some troubling, waiting test, though it was not the key for opening anything, merely for locking up.

She did not want to touch it yet.

She turned back into the hall, where a choice of doors and directions faced her. It did not matter perhaps. She had no particular business in any of the rooms—except the bedroom upstairs, where the business was over. Yet her general and compelling business seemed to be to impregnate with her unseen, unclothed intrusion this house that was and wasn't hers.

And so she did. She glided from room to room. She looked, took in, but also secretly bestowed. She seemed to float on the knowledge that, outrageous as her visiting was—she hadn't a stitch on!—no one would know, guess she had even been here. As if her nakedness conferred on her not just invisibility but an exemption from fact.

Ethel would know of course. But Ethel would think she had been Miss Hobday.

She entered the drawing room. It was like a small deserted foreign country, a collection of pleading but abandoned possessions. As if life itself—she had never had this thought at

Beechwood—was the sum of its possessions. She could not help entering it with the studied deference of a maid announcing a caller or bringing in tea. Yet there was no one there. It was almost like entering those unalterable shrines of the boys' rooms at Beechwood—no need to knock but you felt you should—and she decided at once that she wouldn't go into the equivalent rooms that must be here upstairs. Had she really thought she would? Like this?

The gilt mirror over the mantelpiece suddenly leapt to arrest her, to prove her undeniable, flagrant presence. Look, this is you! You are here!

And had he supposed that *he* was exempt from fact? That a quarter past two might conveniently turn into half past one? She tried to guess the exact calibration of minutes by which his lateness would be merely excused, excused but with frostiness, excused but with hot anger, not excused at all. Not excused, even with the forgiving closeness of their wedding—not excused especially because of that.

She tried to put herself again in the shoes, the skin of Emma Hobday. On the mantelpiece was an invitation, on thick, gold-edged, round-cornered card, expensively printed with scrolling black letters. It was an invitation to Mr. and Mrs. Sheringham from Mr. Hobday and Mrs. Hobday to the wedding of their daughter, Emma Carrington Hobday. It was a formality of course, and had been put there on the mantelpiece simply in proud proclamation. As if they would not have gone to their son's wedding.

"Carrington"?

Returning to the hall, she went to stand before the tall mirror, as though to put herself in her own oddly intangible skin. She had never before had the luxury of so many mirrors. She had never before had the means to view her whole unclad self. All she had in her maid's room was a little square of a mirror, no bigger than one of the hall tiles.

This is Jane Fairchild! This is me!

Paul Sheringham had seen, known, explored this body better than she had done herself. He had "possessed" it. That was another word. He had possessed her body—her body being almost all she possessed. And could it be said that she had possessed and might always possess him?

And had he ever "possessed" Emma Hobday? Well, he would in two weeks.

She tried to picture Emma Hobday's naked body—how it might resemble or not resemble hers. But she couldn't. She couldn't even imagine Emma Hobday without clothes. What was she wearing now, on a March day that was like June? A flowery summer frock? A straw hat? She tried to see Emma Hobday in the mirror. It was even hard to see—though he must have stood before this mirror, a last magnificent look, orchid or no orchid, less than an hour ago—*him*.

Can a mirror keep a print? Can you look into a mirror and see someone else? Can you step through a mirror and *be* someone else?

The grandfather clock chimed two o'clock.

She had not known he was already dead.

SHE TURNED, to consider another choice of doors, and, opening one and then another, found herself in the library. It was not, perhaps, such a random choice. Houses have patterns and proper "houses," even modest ones like Beechwood or

Upleigh, had their libraries. In any case she was glad it was where she found herself to be.

Libraries too—libraries especially—had normally to be entered with much delicate knocking and caution, though as often as not, judging by the one at Beechwood, there was actually no one inside. Yet even when empty they could convey the frowning implication that you should not be there. But then a maid had to dust—and, my, how books could gather dust. Going into the library at Beechwood could be a little like going into the boys' rooms upstairs, and the point of libraries, she sometimes thought, was not the books themselves but that they preserved this hallowed atmosphere of not-to-be-disturbed male sanctuary.

So, few things could be more shocking than for a woman to enter a library naked. The very idea.

The Beechwood library had its wall's worth of books, most of which (a maid knows) had hardly ever been touched. But in one corner, near a buttoned-leather sofa, was a revolving bookcase (she liked to twirl it idly when she was cleaning) in which were kept books that clearly had been read. Surprisingly perhaps, in such a generally grown-up place, they were books that harked back to childhood, boyhood or gathering manhood, books that she imagined might once have flitted between the library and those silent rooms upstairs. There were even a few books that looked newly and hopefully purchased, but never actually begun.

Rider Haggard, G.A. Henty, R.M. Ballantyne, Stevenson, Kipling ... She had good reason to remember the names and even the titles on some of the books. *The Black Arrow, The Coral Island, King Solomon's Mines* ... She would always see their grubby, frayed dust jackets or the exact coloration of their cloth bindings, the wrinklings and fadings of their spines.

Of all the rooms at Beechwood, in fact, the library, for all its dauntingness, was the one she most liked to clean. It was the room in which she most felt like some welcome, innocent thief.

ONE DAY, after she had lodged her bold but shy, even slightly simpering request, Mr. Niven had said, after a lengthy pause for thought, "Well yes, of course you may, Jane." The pause might have suggested that he was permitting some inversion in the hierarchy of the household, or just his puzzlement on a practical point: Well when was she going to read the things, with all her duties to perform? In her sleep? It might have suggested amazement—had the ability not long ago been put to the test—that she could read at all.

But it was nonetheless a yielding, even kindly pause.

"Of course you may, Jane."

They were magic, door-opening words. A different answer—"Who do you think you are, Jane?"—might have undone her life.

It deserved one of her full bobbings. Nothing less.

"But you must let me know which book first. And, of course, you must return it."

"Of course, sir. Thank you very much, sir."

She became a borrower from the Beechwood library, on a carefully monitored yet intrigued, even fostered basis. In fact things took a noticeably sensitive turn with Mr. Niven when it became clear which section of the library she was really interested in. She wouldn't have wanted, after all, to read Foxe's *Book of Martyrs* or Smiles's *Lives of the Engineers* (in five volumes). Who would?

"*Treasure Island*, Jane? What do you want to read *Treasure Island* for? All these books for boys."

It wasn't really a question or query at all, but more like some general bafflement—or a sort of being caught off his guard. He might perhaps have said, with a lot of coughing, "Not those books, Jane. Any books but those."

As for his other observation, well where were the books for girls?

Which she didn't mind at all. Boys' stuff, adventure stuff. She didn't mind not reading girls' stuff, whatever that might be. Adventure. The word itself often loomed and beckoned from the pages: "adventure."

It did not seem that the Nivens of Beechwood, or their kind generally, though they had time and means, were in any way adventurous or even advocates of the idea of adventure. "A jamboree in Henley." Libraries themselves were like dry, sober rejections of adventure. Yet in the Beechwood library was this little spinning cache of stuff that had once, plainly, been gulped down, like an allowable dosage before the onset of tedious or terrible maturity.

Mr. Niven might have said, "Not that book-case please, Jane." But he didn't.

AND LATER, much later in her life, she would say in interviews, in answer to a perennial (and tedious) question, "Oh, boys' books, adventure books, they were the thing. Who would want to read sloppy girls' stuff?"

Her eyes might glint, her wrinkled face purse up a bit more. But then she might say, if she wanted to be less skittish, that reading those books then—"the war, you understand, the first one that is, was barely over"—was like reading across a divide. So close, yet a great divide. Pirates and knights-in-armour, buried treasure and sailing ships. But they were the books she had read.

THE LIBRARY AT Upleigh was remarkably similar. There was the same dominant wall of books that looked as though they had never been read. There were the same small white or black busts—as if from a central warehouse—of men with heavy brows and beards and toga-draped shoulders. There was a desk and, instead of the leather sofa, two dumpy red-brick-coloured armchairs. There was a rack of newspapers and magazines, strange objects of modernity in what might have been a museum. Sunlight came from the window between half-drawn curtains and stretched itself in a bright rectangle over the soft-brown carpet.

On the desk was a small stack of what she rec-ognised as law books. But it was the only sign—it even looked rather arranged—of his supposed intentions while the house was empty and at peace. On a morning like this? Mugging up. She imagined anyway that his diligent studying would have consisted of putting his feet up on the desk and smoking several cigarettes.

She seemed to see him actually doing this, like a ghost in the room. That made two ghosts then. But her ghost was—had been—palpably and unadornedly there. Though no one would ever know.

It was only March, but such was the warmth

that a fly was buzzing and knocking obstinately against the window. And then she saw it, on the other side of the desk: a little enclave of books very similar to the one she knew and had recourse to at Beechwood. She even recognised familiar titles, books she had actually read. So she was not a stranger or trespasser here. In some way she even belonged.

But if Paul Sheringham had ever gone near any of these books, he never said. He gave the impression that he thought there were many things at Upleigh that ought by now to have been chucked away. After all, the bloody horses had all gone. And when she'd told him about her own reading at Beechwood (she wished she hadn't) he'd scoffed, as he scoffed at so many things, and said, "All that tommyrot, Jay? You read all that stuff?" And reminded her at once that their relationship was essentially bodily, physical and here-and-now, it wasn't for droning on about books.

A lawyer? Hardly.

The only difference at Upleigh was that the "boys' books" were not in a separate bookcase, revolving or otherwise, but in a little section (perhaps once cleared of weightier matter) of the main big case, convenient for access.

And the other difference of course was that she was standing naked in the library at Upleigh, something she had never done at Beechwood.

She took one of the books from the shelf in front of her and opened it, and then, for reasons she couldn't have explained, pressed it nursingly to her naked breasts. It was a copy of *Kidnapped*. She knew it. She had read the copy from the bookcase at Beechwood. There was the map of "The Wanderings of David Balfour." There were the words "I will begin the story of my adventures . . ."

She pressed the book to her, then replaced it. No one would know. No one would know about that book's little wandering and adventure. No one would know about the "map" on the sheet upstairs.

SHE LEFT the library. The house's scattered retinue of clocks ticked and whirred. It was the only sound. Outside, the world shone and sang. Here everything was muted, suspended, immured.

She turned into a passage that she instinctively

knew would take her to the stairs to the kitchen. This one, after she descended the stairs, was so still and quiet it might as well have been a library. She felt its unnerving calm. Any kitchen normally has a residual warmth, but this one, beneath the sunny upper floors and left inert all morning, was distinctly cool. But that was her fault perhaps, for wearing no clothes.

Goose bumps emerged on her skin. So too did a vulgar gurgle from her stomach.

The pie, with a knife for cutting it, was on the table, beneath a blue-and-white tea towel. Beside it was a tray with cutlery, napkin, condiments, a bottle of beer and a glass, a bottle opener. The whole collation was presented so that Mister Paul might carry it up to any part of the house if he cared to—the library, for example, so as not to interrupt his studies. That is, if he did not wish to savour the novel experience of eating by himself in the kitchen—and assuming, of course, that he didn't have other plans for passing his time and taking his luncheon.

Who anyway, on a day like this, would really want to bury their nose in a book?

It was a half-pie, a leftover, but, even so, too

much for one. But she attacked it with a sudden ravenous unmannerly hunger. There was no one to watch. He might have done this, she supposed, if the day had turned out differently, if it had followed the course of the pretence he'd invented for it. He might have come down to the kitchen and, suddenly relishing the perverse pleasure of it, wolfed the pie right there at the table. He might have ceased to be the aloof and splendid Paul Sheringham and, with no one to see, become, cheeks bulging, like some guzzling schoolboy or starving tramp.

And she, in her ladylike liberty—and with two and six in her pocket—might have stopped at some village tea shop for egg-and-cress sandwiches and cake.

He must by now be sitting down in his impeccable get-up, with her, at the Swan. Though how might he have accomplished that? By magic? By sheer gall and bravado? "Well, I'm here now . . ." Or readiness to stake everything? "Well, if you want to call it off . . ."

Had that even been his brutal, polished plan? It gave her a brief tingle of hope. To call it off—first clearing his path by causing serious displeasure.

She tried anyway to imagine the scene, even as she chewed on the pie, as he himself, sitting here, might have chewed on it: cheeks crammed, pieces spilling. She wanted to eat this pie, which he hadn't eaten, for him. As if she *were* him.

It was a very good pie. She opened the bottle of beer and drank, if only to wash down the food. It tasted as beer had always tasted the few times she'd drunk it, like brown autumn leaves. She attacked the pie again. Then she felt suddenly like the most miserable and desperate of creatures: no clothes to her back, no roof of her own, and eating someone else's pie.

She shivered. She got to her feet. The pie was too much anyway. She burped loudly. She left everything as it was. She left it, she thought, only as he would have left it—as he had left his discarded clothes. She even turned at the door to see it as if it were all his heedless doing. Ethel would clear it up, of course, later. Ethel or Iris. And it was strange, either of them might think, that he'd eaten the pie, or most of it, if he'd gone to have lunch with Miss Hobday. And if he'd gone to have lunch with Miss Hobday then it was strange that there was also that patch on the sheet.

But Ethel, if it was for her to note both pie and patch, might piece together a story, not unlike one she herself, the Beechwood maid, had fleetingly envisaged. That Miss Hobday, on such a beautiful morning, had taken it upon herself to drive all the way to Upleigh and "surprise" Mister Paul. Meanwhile Mister Paul, toiling at his law books, had got bored and hungry and remembered the veal-and-ham pie. The marauded but unfinished remnants and the barely broached bottle of beer might indeed suggest he had been surprised in his mid-morning raid of the kitchen. And after Miss Hobday's arrival one thing had, unexpectedly or not, led to another, accounting for the stain on the sheet.

And then Mister Paul and Miss Hobday, having taken advantage of the empty house, had left for their lunch, each driving their own car, to preserve the appearance that they had met at their rendezvous. Ethel might even have remembered Mister Paul's saying, on that strange little drive to the station, that he dared say he'd be meeting Miss Hobday for lunch, and then Iris saying that she'd put out a bit of veal-and-ham pie for him anyway, just in case. He wasn't obliged of course to discuss his plans with the servants, and it was peculiar if he did. But then his personally taking them to the station was rather peculiar too.

It was a peculiar day.

Ethel, she supposed later, might have constructed such a story, and she might even have seen, when the time came, how her story had its failings. But much the greater likelihood was that Ethel, when attending to one or both messes, would not have thought very much about either of them, or their nefarious implications, it not being her business to think about such things. She had enough to think about anyway, having just been to her mother's.

Would Ethel even have thought, or would Iris, who had much more to do with the pie: Well if he ate the pie, it was the last meal he ate?

SHE ASCENDED the stairs. There was another kind of popular book besides the boys' adventure book and one even favoured by adults. But she would say, in her interviews, that she had never had much time for the detective story. For reading them—let alone writing them. Life itself was riddle enough.

She climbed up from the kitchen into the warmth and light of the upper floors. And now, though she had no actual need to hurry—the clock in the hall said twenty past two and the world was still at lunch—she wished to leave, she had explored sufficiently.

It was then anyway (so she would always know the exact timing of its ringing) that the telephone—or a telephone—rang from some nearby recess she hadn't previously noticed. She froze. She had the odd sensation that it had rung because she'd moved close to it. She didn't answer it anyway, it would have been foolish to answer it, though she was quite good at answering telephones. Its ringing went on for some time while she stood stock-still, as if, had she moved, the telephone might somehow have observed her, which was foolish too.

But wasn't it utterly foolish anyway to be standing here in this unfamiliar hall with nothing on?

She climbed the staircase and re-entered the bedroom. It was the same, of course it was, as she had left it. Only the sun, still flooding in, had lowered its angle a little. There was the open window, the clothes over the armchair, his unwanted trousers, still scarfed with one of her stockings. The pulled-back bedclothes. The patch, a little drier. Yet it seemed like a room round which, even in such a short interval, some invisible fence had been raised. Was it really the room in which . . . ? Was it really here that . . . ?

It was the profoundest of questions. Had it really happened?

Beyond the window the birds chirped eternally and in the blue sky she could not see, or would not remember seeing, any flaw.

The mirror on the dressing table offered its last three-fold glimpse of her nakedness. She put on her clothes. They slipped on like some much-used disguise. She touched—only to touch, to stroke, not to tidy—his trousers. She didn't close the open window. Again, as he might have carelessly left it. Ethel's job. And who anyway was going to come with a ladder . . . ? She did not touch the bed, even to cover the patch.

The young men in their frames on the dressing table seemed now oblivious of her. Was it all her vain fancy that they had previously peeped? They looked immovably through her, at some camera that had clicked long ago. She stood in the doorway and took her own last mental photograph. Then left.

In the hall she paused again and took— plucked—one of the orchid flowers from the clusters above the bowl. Well, if he hadn't, she would. She realised at once that it would be the most incriminating of items, if she were to wear it. If she were to return to Beechwood with an orchid stuck in her frock. But it wasn't for wearing. She slipped it where earlier in the day she had slipped her half-crown. It would get quickly bruised and tattered perhaps, but it was her proof to herself. It was so she herself would always know. No one else ever would.

ADVENTURE STORIES, not detective stories. Boys' books. They were the thing. And her interviewer might say, treating it all as a bit of a joke and not anyway wanting the interview to get too "booky": "And boys themselves?"

"Oh yes," she would say with an away-with-you flip of her eighty-year-old hand, as if there had once been queues. The audience in their darkened seats might titter obligingly. And the interviewer might not even see, amid the playfulness, the brief narrowing of the eyes at the change of subject.

It was that life itself might be an adventure. That was the submerged message (the "subtext" they might say now) of all those books. Was there in fact any other way to live? And adventure did not have to be about pirates and narrow escapes. It might be a constant mental hazarding. Suppose, imagine. Imagine. What did writers do with their time? They were the most unadventurous souls on earth, weren't they? Sitting all day at their desks.

But she would not say such things in interviews. Only, with her protective twinkle and ironically squeezed lips, skirt teasingly round their intimate truth.

I will begin the story of my adventures . . .

SHE PUT the key under the chunk of stone pineapple. She could not see how Freddy could have broken it with a cricket bat. A battle-axe possibly. And she did not know which one was Freddy in the silver frames. She might have asked, she ought to have asked, but she hadn't. "Which one is which? Tell me about them." Would it have been the moment, lying there together? Or would he have fended off the question, a look on his face of having tasted something bad?

Now she would never know.

There, against the wall, was her bicycle, her potentially incriminating bicycle that had incriminated no one. She steered it for a while across the gravel before mounting, drawing deep unsteady breaths. She was slightly sore where she met the saddle. She tucked and gathered her skirt. The air was warm and bright and brimming round her.

A sudden unexpected freedom flooded her. Her life was beginning, it was not ending, it had not ended. She would never be able to explain (or be required to) this illogical, enveloping inversion. As if the day had turned inside out, as if what she was leaving behind was not enclosed, lost, entombed in a house. It had merged somehow— pouring itself outwards—with the air she was breathing. She would never be able to explain it, and she would not feel it any the less even when she discovered, as she would do, how this day had turned really inside out. Could life be so cruel yet so bounteous at the same time?

She rode off. She did not ride—as he'd departed and she'd arrived—along the drive to the gate and the road. Old habit and old secrecy made her take the old route. Past the stables, through the rhododendrons, past the vegetable plot, the potting shed, the cold frames and greenhouse, then along mere threading paths and through narrow gaps between neglected shrubs into a jumbled outer region that led to a copse. Every twist and turn, every screening outbuilding and clump of vegetation was familiar to her. They had met among them and made use of them often enough. It was even his standard directive: "the garden path."

The secret back route from Beechwood to Upleigh would remain always in her head, such that she might at any time have easily drawn its map, like the map in *Treasure Island* or of David Balfour's wanderings in the Highlands. She would retain the ability, but of course it would be a contradiction, a betrayal, actually to draw a secret map.

"The garden path, Jay." And, once, with a strange echoing sincerity, "I won't ever lead you up it."

The copse led to a small wilderness of rough grass and brambles, then a straggly hedgerow, where there was another way out of what was still Upleigh land. It involved lifting the bicycle fully over a stile, but she had done it enough times. She might, of course, have left the bicycle—it was her usual practice—safely hidden in the hedgerow. But his crisp command had simply empowered her. The front door.

Beyond the hedgerow—it was dense and spreading at this point and it seemed that even in the space of hours the hawthorns had sprouted more green leaves and more white frothing blossom—there was the curve of a narrow minor road. Once on its surface, she could speed anywhere, a mere carefree wayfarer, out pedalling on a heavenly Sunday afternoon.

Though for a crippling moment she didn't know which way to turn. It must have been perhaps three o'clock. She had half the after-noon yet. To turn left would have been the quickest way back to Beechwood, so the obvious choice was right. But where to? Pushing off, she decided that it didn't matter, the main thing was simply to be riding, careering through this warm exhilarating air, and since the road to the right took her down a long sunny swoop then up a gentle rise (it was the back of the Upleigh grounds) her decision, to be indecisive, was confirmed.

Pedalling hard at first, then freewheeling and gathering speed, she heard the whirr of the wheels, felt the air fill her hair, her clothes and almost, it seemed, the veins inside her. Her veins sang, and she herself might have sung, if the rushing air had not stopped her mouth. She would never be able to explain the sheer liberty, the racing sense of possibility she felt. All over the country, maids and cooks and nannies had been "freed" for the day, but was any of them—was even Paul Sheringham—as untethered as she?

Could she have done what she'd done today

if she'd had a mother to go to? Could she have had the life she didn't yet know she was going to have? Could her mother have known, making her dreadful choice, how she had blessed her?

And, like a mother to herself, she would never forget that girl on a bicycle, though she would never mention her to anyone, never breathe a word.

Girl? She was twenty-two. The air up her skirt and a Dutch cap up her fanny.

BEYOND THE TOP of the rise was a crossroads with one of those four-fingered country signposts, black on white. She might have taken any direction and ridden off for ever. She had her hidden treasure. She had taken a secret munch of pie and swig of ale in that house over there, behind the trees!

But she stopped for a long time at the crossroads. Three o'clock. At Henley now, puddings finished, they might be reflecting on the forthcoming event. Mr. Hobday would have established his benign authority over the assembly and Mr. Niven might have become hopeful that he would not have to share the bill. Meanwhile at Bollingford the subjects of their rosy considerations might have passed miraculously—who knows?—beyond the moment of almost terminal conflagration. Fireworks quenched by champagne. Emma Hobday might have succumbed to Paul Sheringham's impregnable poise. "Must we, Emsie? On a day like this? Just because I was half an hour late ... All right, forty minutes. What's ten minutes?" His hand, by now, finding her knee.

Is that how it might have gone after all? All the scenes. Suppose.

She stood, one foot on the verge, the other on a pedal. There was not a murmur, in any direction, of traffic. There was only the birdsong and, in the warm air, the half-heard stirring and rousing of—everything. Spring.

She took the left turn, only, after a mile or so, to take another left turn. It was a circuitous way back to Beechwood. She had still half the afternoon, yet she knew, now, what she wanted to do with her remaining time.

It was what she might have done anyway, what she might have said to Mr. Niven, had not circumstances happily dictated otherwise. Or she might have just set off on this bicycle, with a sandwich from Milly and two and six, and found some sunny quiet spot. To sit, to lie, with her bicycle and her book. It was a book by Joseph Conrad. She'd never heard of him. She'd only just begun it.

She might have brought the book with her, she thought, so she might have had it now. But that was absurd. The front door, with her Dutch cap—and a book to read! But she might, all along—had not the telephone triumphantly rung—have said that thing about just sitting in the garden with a book.

"If I may, Mr. Niven."

And he might have said, imagining the rather charming scene, "Of course you may, Jane."

Well, now she would finish her day, her Mothering Sunday, as it might have begun.

And so it was that in order to keep an appointment with a book—with Joseph Conrad—she turned left, then left again, making her way back to Beechwood earlier than needed, though, even so, not directly or quickly. She might still enjoy this glorious sunshine and the thrill of being so fully alive in it, on a whirring, whizzing bicycle. She might still stamp the memory of it on herself for ever.

And so it was that she reached Beechwood some while after four, only to discover that Mr. and Mrs. Niven had, surprisingly, already returned. There was Mr. Niven, as she rode up the drive, standing on the gravel beside the Humber, almost as she had last seen him that morning, though clearly, as she drew near him, in a very different frame of mind. And saying, "Jane. Is that you, Jane?"

What a strange thing to say. Was she someone else?

"Jane, is that you—back so early? I have some distressing news."

ONE DAY, when it had long been her business—her profession, even the reason why she was "well known"—to write stories and to deal intricately with words, she would be asked another perennial and somewhat tedious question: "So when—so how did you become a writer?" She had answered it enough times and, really, you couldn't answer it in a different way every time. Yet people—surprisingly since her occupation was telling stories—did not jump to the conclusion that in giving her standard answer, she might also be telling a story, only kidding, as it were. They took her at her word. And, after all, it was a good answer, a fairly unchallengeable one.

"At birth. At birth, of course," she would say, even when she was asked this question in her seventies or eighties or nineties, when her birth, always a mysterious fact, now seemed the remotest and strangest of events.

"I was an orphan," she would divulge for the umpteenth time. "I never knew my father or mother. Or even my real name. If I ever had one. That has always seemed to me the perfect basis for becoming a writer—particularly a writer of fiction. To have no credentials at all. To be given a clean sheet, or rather, to *be* a clean sheet yourself. A nobody. How can you become a somebody without first being a nobody?"

And a characteristic glint might enter her eye, an additional crease appear at the corner of her mouth, and her interviewer might think that, yes, there was a touch of slyness here. Jane Fairchild was known for being a crafty old bird. But the gaze, for all the glinting, was steady, the face, for all its knottiness, essentially straight. It even seemed to be putting the innocent counter-question: You think I would tell you a lie?

"Not just an orphan," she might go on, "but a foundling. Now there's a word for you. Not such a common one, is it, these days? Foundling. It sounds like a word from the eighteenth century. Or from a fairy tale. But I was left on the steps of an orphanage—in some sort of bundle, I suppose—and taken in. That is what I was told. There were places in those days where that sort of thing could happen. 1901. It was a differ-ent world. Not the start in life any of us might wish for. But then in some ways"—the glint would appear again—"the perfect one.

"My name, Fairchild, was one of the names

that were given to foundling children. There were lots of Fairchilds, Goodchilds, Goodbodys and so on who came out of orphanages—so that they would have, I suppose, a well-intentioned start in life. People sometimes ask me—goodness knows why—do I write under my own name, my real name? Well yes I do—it was my given name. Jane Fairchild. But it might as well be a pen name. I might as well call myself Jane Foundling. In fact, it has a rather pleasing ring, don't you think?"

"And the Jane?"

"Oh Jane is just any old girl's name, isn't it? Young girl's, I mean. Jane Austen, Jane Eyre, Jane Russell . . ."

And so, with a gleam in her eye and a tightening of her lips, she would suggest she had come into the world with an innate licence to invent. And with an intimate concern for how words attach to things.

"My birthright, so to speak. If you'll pardon the pun."

But she would never disclose that when she really became a writer, or had the seed of it truly planted in her (and that was an interesting word, "seed") was one very warm day in March, when she was twenty-two and she had wandered round a house without a shred on—naked, you might say, as on the day she was born—and had felt both more herself, more Jane Fairchild, than she'd ever felt before, yet also, as never before, like some visiting ghost. Had felt, you might say, what it truly means to be put down in this world, placed, so to speak, on its extraordinary doorstep.

And how, after all, could you admit to such things in a public interview (sprightly as some of her interviews could be): I wandered naked round a house that wasn't even mine, that I'd never even entered before. And how did I get to be doing that? Well there was a whole story there, a story she'd sworn to herself never to tell. Nor had she. Nor would she.

Though here she was, look, a storyteller by trade.

IT WAS Mothering Sunday 1924. A different thing from the nonsense they call Mother's Day now. And she had no mother, you see.

She was raised in an orphanage, then put into service. Another phrase you don't hear often these days, but another "start in life" she would recommend to the would-be writer (though it was hardly to be recommended in 1980 or 1990). Since it made you an occupational observer of life, it put you on the outside looking in. Since those who served served, and those who were being served—lived. Though sometimes, to be honest, it felt at the time entirely the other way round. It was the servants who lived, and a hard life they had of it, and the ones who were served who seemed not to know exactly what to do with their lives. Proper lost souls, in fact, some of them . . .

She'd been put into service at fourteen. Two years later, in 1917, she'd gone to Beechwood House in Berkshire. She'd been "taken in" once again, you might say, by Mr. and Mrs. Niven, whose family had been recently reduced by the loss of two sons, and who required in those hard-pressed wartime years only a novice maid (meaning perhaps simply cheap) in addition to their existing cook.

Out of motives best known to themselves— though not so difficult to fathom perhaps—they had considered and chosen an orphan, and then discovered that the poor forlorn thing was not so lacking in spark or gumption at all. It turned out she could read, more than many maids could, more than the word "Brasso" on a tin, and could write more than a shopping list, and could do sums.

"Can you tell me, Jane, what are three and six plus seven and six?"

"Eleven shillings, Mr. Niven, sir."

She was half educated.

It even emerged one day that she wanted to read books. Books! And instead of its seeming a damned cheek, it had only stirred further the charitable urges already present in the house. It had only touched some capacity for paternal leniency in Mr. Niven that this orphan girl— this Fairchild—should be allowed to borrow books from his library.

When he learned which kind of book she preferred he might have gently but firmly protested, but perhaps her preference only brought out the leniency all the more. Mr. Niven sometimes disappeared into the library himself. It was what, she sometimes thought, libraries were for: for men to disappear into and be important in, even though they had disappeared. She sometimes thought Mr. Niven went into the library to cry.

The leniency extended to her own occasional "disappearances." Mr. and Mrs. Niven had no complaints about her work generally—the opposite—but she could now and then be oddly absent—beyond, that is, her designated days and half-days off. As when she seemed to take for ever over simple shopping errands. Or those times she said she had a puncture, or her chain had come off again (there seemed to be a curse on the Second Bicycle) and she'd had to seek the kind help of other passing cyclists. But then there were times—true, usually in the quieter stretches of the day—when she was simply not to be found.

Though now perhaps these absences could be explained. She had snatched a moment in her room, not, as once fondly supposed, to bemoan in private her sad orphan's lot, but to read a book.

You could hardly allow her to borrow books and then not allow her at least some time to read them. And the house was not any more, let's face it, as in the old days, a firmly governed, a strictly regimented house. Look where regimentation had got the world.

Had Mr. Niven, had either of them, ever wondered, guessed?

OH YES, she would say, the glint in her eye, she was lucky to have been born with nothing to her name. With not even a name, in fact. Or the real date of her birth. So she was not only nameless, but ageless. And her eighty-year-old face would bloom.

The first of May was the date of birth that had been accorded to her, by rough approximation and perhaps because it was a nice date, just as Jane Fairchild was a nice name. Some mothers, apparently, left a little note, inside the bundle, with just a date of birth and a name. Only the first name. The commoner the better. No one ever deposited a Laetitia. And, if you thought about it, the name must have only been a thought anyway. And wasn't any name just a thought? Why was a tree called a tree?

She might even have liked to be called Jane Bundle.

And did it matter if you marked your birthday on the wrong day? If it had really been the 25th of April, though you never knew. The wrong day became the right day. This was the great truth of life, that fact and fiction were always merging, interchanging. And if you were a maid you weren't given much leisure to mark your birthday anyway—if anyone even knew it. You weren't given the day off. And being a maid was a little like being an orphan, since you lived in someone else's house, you didn't have a home of your own to go to.

Except on Mothering Sunday. When you did get the day off, to go home to your family. Which would always put her at a bit of a loss. What to do, what to do with herself on Mothering Sunday? She could hardly go looking for her mother.

Though what would she have done with herself anyway, with her life, if she hadn't been a maid? And she supposed—the furrowed face would bloom again—that it was a very common human predicament. To be at a loss, not to know what to do with yourself.

"MY YEARS AS a maid," she would call them, "my maid's years," never adding, "but not for long my maidenly ones." "My years in service." It was hard to think now of a time when half the world was "in service." She was born in 1901—at least the year must have been right—and she would grow up to become a maid, which anyone might have predicted. But to become a writer— no one could have predicted that. Not even the kindly committee at the orphanage who had re-conceived her as Jane Fairchild, born on the first of May. And, least of all perhaps, her mother.

When she was asked, in the interviews, to describe the atmosphere of those wartime years (meaning, of course, the First War), she would say that it was so long ago now and so like another world that trying to remember it was a bit like—writing a novel. Had she really been alive then? But if she were honest she would add that she'd been not unaware of it, of course—all that accumulated loss and grief. How could anyone be unaware of it? Every week she dusted two rooms where everything was to remain "just as it was." You went in, took a little breath perhaps, and got on with it.

But she had never known them, the boys who'd had those rooms, and what she mainly thought was: A whole room, full of furniture, *each*. And if you had yourself been comprehensively bereaved at birth—and that was her situation, wasn't it?—how could you share in all that stuff, how could you have anything left over for it? The war wasn't her fault, was it? And, yes, you might say she was lucky, not to have a brother or father, let alone, at that age, a husband to think about. And, yes, you might say it was her good luck to have been raised in a good orphanage, they weren't all evil places rife with abuse. Her mother, whoever she was, had perhaps had some discernment.

So she'd received a rudimentary education

when many who had parents didn't. When many who were packed off to the trenches didn't. She'd been put into service at fourteen with a relatively advanced ability to read and write and— free from all family ties—with perhaps more than a usual eagerness for life.

And who wouldn't want to be Jane Fairchild, born on the first of May?

Oh yes—the face would flower again—she was very fortunate to have been born destitute.

"ARE YOU an orchid, Jane?" Cook Milly had said, after first looking at her very closely, not long after she'd arrived, as if to establish precisely what sort of specimen she would have to work with. "Because my mother was an orchid too."

Had she really said it? And if so, had she used that word deliberately and knowingly— knowing that she was using the wrong word, not the right one? There was a look of purest artlessness and candour in Cook Milly's eye. And did it matter if she'd used the wrong word—if the wrong word was a better one? It would have been wrong to point out that she had made a mistake—to expose, at such a moment, Milly's poor grasp of language and lack of education, while asserting her own accomplishment. That is, if it was a mistake.

And if you were an orphan, then perhaps you might turn into an orchid, as Cinderella turned into a princess.

Had she really said it? Or had she herself misheard it? Or invented this little exchange between herself and Milly? Even then? Surely not. The great truth of life. So that one day she might go on to invent a whole character— a minor but colourful character in her novel *Tell Me Again* (she actually thought of calling her Milly Cook)—who was given to using misapprehended words. Who said "cucumbered" when she meant "encumbered." And in fact the real and living Cook Milly became more and more, in the course of those "maid's years" at Beechwood and certainly by the time of that Mothering Sunday, like some cook in a story book, plump and sturdy and red-cheeked, with thick forearms meant for commanding a mixing bowl.

But what had mattered most—and was strangely clear—was that Cook Milly, who was only three years her elder, was implicitly proposing to be her, Jane Fairchild's, mother—her substitute mother—for the duration. And such was the sincerity that flowed out of Milly that she, the new, disoriented maid, could not help but at once implicitly accept this offer. And never disown it, even though it would emerge that she was a good deal sharper than Cook Milly, so that Milly, who did not have an ounce of cleverness or cunning in her, might be seen as the child of the two of them.

Yet she would always wonder if she had really meant to say "orchid." And how much she might have known, guessed all along, about her and Paul Sheringham.

She would call the character, after all, Molly Cook. And the duration—of her adoption, as it were, by Milly—would be seven years, since within six months of that Mothering Sunday Cook Milly, who had always had her eccentricities with words, went more seriously funny in the head and was taken away to some place (she never knew where, if it wasn't her own poor mother's) where women of her station and condition got taken, never to return.

So she was orphaned, you might say, a second time.

And what if orphans really were called orchids? And if the sky was called the ground. And if a tree was called a daffodil. Would it make any difference to the actual nature of things? Or their mystery?

And what if she had not stayed on the bed but had gone down the stairs with him, still naked, her cool feet on the cool chessboard tiles, to take an orchid from the bowl and hold it to his lapel?

"For me. Since we will never meet again."

Like some far-fetched scene in a far-fetched story book.

SHE WOULD BECOME a writer, and because she was a writer, or because it was what had made her become a writer, be constantly beset by the inconstancy of words. A word was not a thing, no. A thing was not a word. But somehow the two—things—became inseparable. Was everything a great fabrication? Words were like an invisible skin, enwrapping the world and giving it reality. Yet you could not say the world would not be there, would not be real if you took away the words. At best it seemed that things might bless the words that distinguished them, and that words might bless everything.

But she would never say these things in interviews.

She would sometimes discuss them—even discuss them in bed—with her husband Donald Campion. She would call him the Great Dissector. And he would call her the Great Vivisector. Now, there was a word. And she would poke her tongue out at him.

"And what other things do you think are necessary for becoming a writer?"

"Well, you have to understand that words are only words, just bits of air . . ."

The crow's feet round her eyes positively dancing.

"OH, ADVENTURE STORIES, of course, boys' stories. In spite of the fact that there was still a war going on and all that boys' stuff had become sheer nonsense. Sheer tommyrot."

"And—boys themselves?"

"You mean—adventures *with* boys . . . ?"

SHE WOULD BECOME a writer. She would live to be ninety-eight. She would live to have seen two world wars and the reigns of four kings and one queen. And very nearly two queens, since she must have been begotten—only just—in the reign of Queen Victoria. "Begotten, then forgotten."

She was ten years old and in an orphanage when a big ship hit an iceberg, making some more orphans. She was twelve years old when a woman threw herself under a king's horse. She had just turned fifteen when she worked for a while, one summer, in a big house—she had never seen such a palace—and learnt all about nocturnal emissions.

She would live to be almost as old as the century and to know she had probably known and seen—and written—enough. She did not mind, she would cheerfully say, if she did not make it to the year 2000. It was a wonder she had made it this far. Her life had "19" written on it and nineteen was a good age to be. Her face would bloom.

Not that it was really so much—the knowing and seeing—even in seventy, eighty, ninety years. "Her maid's years," "her Oxford years," "her London years," "her Donald years." You lived in your own little cranny, didn't you? All those years at a desk! Even her years of so-called fame, of being shunted around the world, being in places she would never have dreamed of being in—they had all gone by in a blur. And then it was "Jane Fairchild at Seventy," "Jane Fairchild at Seventy-five," "Jane Fairchild at Eighty." For heaven's sake! And batting away the same old questions.

But if you counted what she had seen in her mind's eye. Well then ... All the places, all the scenes. *In the Mind's Eye*: it was the title of her most well-known book. And could she disentangle it, the stuff she'd seen in her mind's eye, from the actual stuff of her own life? Well, of course she bloody well could, she wasn't a fantasist.

And of course she bloody well couldn't. It was the whole point of being a writer, wasn't it, to embrace the stuff of life? It was the whole point of *life* to embrace it.

"HER OXFORD YEARS"! That was a case in point. Yes, she'd gone to Oxford. She could truly say that, but not in the way, of course, some people could say it. Yet she would love to say gaily and freely in interviews, "Oh yes, I was at Oxford . . ." "When I was at Oxford . . ."

Yes, she had gone to Oxford, in October 1924, to work as an assistant in a bookshop, Paxton's Bookshop in Catchpole Lane. And books, she knew by then, were one of the necessities, the rocks of her life.

It was her first job after being a maid and the first big step in life she had taken for herself. Not a big step, you might think, from maid to shop girl, but it had required some initiative and daring, even some writerly skill, in answering the advert. And it had required Mr. Niven's cooperation in writing her a reference. Perhaps he had said that she'd made more use of his own library than he had.

In any case she had got the job. And Mr. Niven must have understood what a big step it was for her and that she was fully determined to take it, since when she left he gave her ten pounds (ten pounds!) with which to set herself up in Oxford. And she had anyway the money she'd saved from her maid's wages (not having a family that had any call on them), not to mention from the occasional half-crowns and florins Mr. Niven would bestow on her.

Mr. Niven had learnt economy, but there were still the vestiges of largesse.

By this time Milly had left and there was a new cook called Winifred, and there would soon be a new maid too. And she, Jane Fairchild, would never know what became of Beechwood or Upleigh. She would never go back. It was almost a superstition. Some things, some places perhaps take up their truer existence in the mind. Even when she had a car—especially when she had a car—she would never go back, even just to drive by, to stop and look and wonder.

She went to Oxford, to work for Mr. Paxton. She was only an assistant in a bookshop, but an able one, increasingly familiar with books and—what perhaps mattered most—very good with customers, who ranged from mere towns-folk to the cream of the university, even professors. It soon became clear to Mr. Paxton that he had acquired an asset. And it became clear soon enough too that the increasing familiarity with books went with an increasing familiarity with the customers.

The fact was that she began to consort, to go out, even to go to bed with some of them, and it wouldn't have been wrong to say that this is what she had hoped, even vaguely foreseen. If she couldn't have "gone to Oxford" in the other sense, then she became intimate with those who had. It might even be said that she moved in university "circles" even more freely and successfully than many—poor swots that they were—who were actually *there*. She could even pass herself off quite convincingly as that rare and frightening creature, a female undergraduate.

"And what are you studying?"

"Studying? Oh no, I'm just a shop girl."

It was remarkable how their eyes might light up.

And later on she might dare to say, "I'm a shop girl, but—I write too."

One day, in the little back office, Mr. Paxton, close observer of all this and committed family man, had said, "I'm going to get a new typewriter, Jane. This thing has seen better days." There was an awkwardly stoical look in his eye as if he might have been talking about himself. The old typewriter was perfectly serviceable.

"Would you like it?" he said.

And that, you might say, was when she really became a writer. The third time. As well as at birth. As well as one fine day in March, when she was a maid.

HER OXFORD DAYS! Her Oxford years! Oh, they were great days. She saw Oxford all right. It was an education. And, to be perfectly honest, she was sometimes in some respects the educator. Even of some of the best brains in the land. How many, in Oxford? Oh, she couldn't remember now. And of course it was in Oxford that she met her husband, Donald Campion. But that was a whole other story. It was funny how you could say even of life itself: That was another story.

"It wasn't the smoothest of marriages, was it? You and Donald Campion?"

"What makes you say that?"

"Well—two minds. Two careers. He was the bright young philosopher, wasn't he?"

She didn't say, "It was a thing of bodies too." Though at eighty she might have got away with it. If the truth be known—but Donald himself had never known it—Donald had reminded her of Paul Sheringham. And she certainly wasn't going to reveal that in an interview.

"You mean there wouldn't have been room for both his books and mine?" But she didn't say that either. She could clam up sometimes just as effectively as she could quip. What a good mask it was, being turned eighty, with a face like a squeezed-out dish mop.

"And—so tragically short." Her interviewer blundered on.

"Donald or the marriage?" But she didn't say that either.

"Yes, it was tragic," she said, with a voice like flint. And didn't say, as she might have done—at eighty she could be oracular: We are all fuel. We are born, and we burn, some of us more quickly than others. There are different kinds of combustion. But not to burn, never to catch fire at all, that would be the sad life, wouldn't it?

But she'd said it anyway, or something like it, in a book somewhere. And if the truth be known, grief at Donald's death, the second grief of her life, was like the end of her own life. She might have jumped on his pyre. Instead of which she became a better and famous writer.

In the Mind's Eye. It wasn't published, it wasn't finished—in some ways, it wasn't even *begun*—till after Donald was taken away from her in the autumn of 1945 by a brain tumour. His bleak joke was that he'd been too brainy. Another was that there'd be no chance now of his breaking any Secrets Act. He had safely survived the war as a code-breaker, and his best work was perhaps still to come. It would all now, she thought—her own bleak joke—be like a work of fiction.

"We had the same quandary, you know, Donald and I. Words and things."

She had toyed with *All in the Mind*. She had even toyed with *Secrets Act*. But fancy publishing a novel called that. *In the Mind's Eye . . . All in the Mind* . . . Either way, it sounded abstract, even rather cerebral. Ha! Twelve years the wife of a philosopher.

In fact it was her most physical, her most carnal, her most downright *sexual* book. She had found a way, at last, of writing about all that *stuff.* And it was her first big success. She was forty-eight, not so old (there are some mercies) for a writer, but too old to be the mother that, for her own reasons, she'd always shied away from being. You might say she was given no good examples in motherhood. Except Milly. Now, with Donald and his blue-grey gaze and his rat-a-tat laugh gone, she wished she'd yielded.

Forty-eight and famous. *In the Mind's Eye.* Some people were shocked and scandalised. It was only 1950. It would look tame in twenty years' time. And she was—to make it worse—a "lady novelist." A lady novelist? Where did they get that phrase from? And where did they think she came from?

Forty-eight and famous and widowed and childless and not yet halfway through her orphaned life.

"I HAVE SOME distressing news."

Even as Mr. Niven spoke, words displayed their fickle ability to fly away from things. Such was his evident struggle to find words and such her recent experience that she thought he'd said "undressing news." I have some undressing news. A mistake that even Milly couldn't have made.

And when, after he'd got more words out, he said, "You have gone very pale, Jane," she had the fleeting thought that it was surely something people only did in books. People only "went pale" or had "faces of thunder" or eyes that "flashed fire" or blood that "ran cold" in books. Books that she had read.

"I'm so sorry, Jane, to be telling you this. On Mothering Sunday."

As if his presence—it seemed now that he was alone—back here at Beechwood at this hour was expressly to deliver news meant for her. As if he had come with the unexpected information that she had no mother.

"There has been an accident, Jane. A fatal accident. Involving Paul Sheringham. Mister Paul at Upleigh."

She had the presence of mind, or mere mumbling reflex, to say, "At Upleigh?"

"No, Jane, not at Upleigh. A road accident. A car accident."

That was when he said, "You have gone very pale, Jane." It even seemed that he was stepping forward, arms held out, a little hesitantly but gallantly, because he thought she might be going to faint.

SHE WOULD NEVER know how Mr. Niven might have recorded his own version of this scene and all that followed. How he might have "written it," as it were. She would never know—but this was surely her own sudden panicky surmise—how much he *knew*.

She would never know (even at seventy or eighty) how much other people—people who weren't writers—did any of this stuff. It was a mystery.

Paul Sheringham didn't. She would have said she was sure of that. And that was—had been—his glory.

He had driven off (as she knew) when, unless some sorcery, some suspension of the laws of physics occurred, he would have been late. She knew (though she would never tell anyone) that he had made no effort to hurry—the opposite—though he was going to meet his bride-to-be. But he had made every effort, nonetheless, to prepare himself immaculately. This too only she would ever truly know, since after the impact the car had caught fire and his body was not only mangled but burnt. But items survived, she would learn, to suggest his state of attire—and his identity. An initialled cigarette case, a signet ring. The car itself was not so destroyed that it could not be readily identified as the car Paul Sheringham (often with some verve) drove.

But he would anyway have been significantly late. So that Emma Hobday's at first trivial but then intensifying feelings of bafflement, anger and indignation might have turned eventually into appalling conjecture. Good God—she had simply been stood up! Her husband-to-be had chosen this day—this marvellous day—to isolate her while he made his getaway. Law studies indeed! He had seized the opportunity of the house being completely deserted to—desert her! To drive off into the blue yonder. Because he could not face—it was only two weeks—marrying his betrothed wife. Or any other of his looming obligations. And this was his monstrous way of announcing it.

In short, she was being royally jilted. And, while she knew that her outraged imagination might just be getting the better of her and she could be becoming hysterical, some part of her—which knew Paul Sheringham—yet thought: And it might be just like him.

And so . . .

But only she, perhaps, Jane Fairchild, the maid at Beechwood, would "write" this scene. Emma Hobday wasn't a character in a book, was she? She hadn't invented her. She would never know how Emma Hobday herself might have written it.

And so . . . And so Miss Hobday couldn't just sit there, looking at her dainty wristwatch, could she, and being looked at by others? Her stomach unpleasantly rumbling. She had asked to use the hotel's telephone. This was all so unthinkable and embarrassing. But she was now at the centre of a world that was betraying her, undoing her appointed future. She had called first Upleigh House. No answer. The ringing telephone even seemed to be saying: This house is empty, there is no one here, no one listening. So then!

And then, after pacing this way and that and biting her lip, even going outside to draw deep breaths and look in all directions, and struggling with the thought that she really was behaving insanely, she had called the police. Perhaps the police might actually chase—chase and capture—her escaping fiancé, or come up with some other explanation that might at least save her from total ignominy.

And so, by that time of day, with information they by then would have had, the police would have had no alternative but to answer her enquiry and, yes, at least to save her from ignominy.

And so a further rapid and terrible succession of telephone calls had followed. The Swan at Bollingford was now ministering to a shocked woman who yet could still impart some vital details. Yes, the George Hotel at Henley. Further down the river. That's where they'd all gone, that's where they'd all be.

If they hadn't actually decided on some picnic. Or if they weren't, even now, on a sudden whim, cruising gaily and unreachably along the Thames on a hired launch. It had all been going to be like a sunny saluting of the imminent marriage—from which the happy couple themselves had judiciously excused themselves. If only they had meekly signed up to it.

But fortunately they were all still at the George, even still at their lunch table, still toying with sherry trifles.

And so everyone's day had changed utterly.

And so Mr. Niven had driven back here on his own, for reasons he was yet fully to explain. Though those can't have been—she might still have been anywhere, even by the banks of the Thames herself, enjoying her motherless Mothering Sunday—to announce it all to her.

"Jane, would you like to sit down?"

The only place would have been inside the Humber. Like Ethel and Iris. But she wasn't going to faint. She was still clutching the handlebars of her bicycle.

ALL THE AVAILABLE EVIDENCE was that— whatever had detained him—he was trying to minimise his lateness. He must have been driving fast at any rate. And he had taken the minor road which, though narrower and twistier, was a short cut, crossing the railway line by a bridge and so avoiding the level-crossing on the main road, which it might have been just his luck to find shut against him.

But he never crossed the railway line.

He was known to be a sometimes speedy yet

knowledgeable user of the local lanes. So he would certainly have known about the short cut—if you were heading for Bollingford—and known about the distinct right-hand bend the road made half a mile or so before the railway bridge. It was more of a corner in fact, indicating perhaps where surveyors and landowners had once failed to agree. There was even a large oak on the apex of the bend, marking the hazard. And Paul Sheringham had driven straight into it.

It was bright sunshine, a glorious day. There was no possibility that he had not *seen* the bend, the approaching, still leafless oak. There were road signs anyway. And he must have taken this bend scores of times. Perhaps his brakes had failed. The condition of the car could never reveal this. Perhaps—since no other traffic was involved—some innocent yet fatal factor, such as a stray farm animal, was responsible. Though would you crash into a tree to avoid a lesser, if significant, mishap?

The conclusion, even the formal verdict of an inquest, would be that a terrible—a "tragic"—accident had occurred. And this conclusion was reached not just from lack of witnesses or evidence to the contrary, but because it was the conclusion that everyone—the Sheringhams and Hobdays particularly, who had considerable connections with local officialdom—wished to reach. No one wished to believe that, two weeks before his marriage to Miss Emma Hobday and while actually driving to meet her, Paul Sheringham had driven fatally into a tree for any other reason than that it was an accident.

Mr. Sheringham senior would no doubt have explained, when asked, that because of the peculiarity of the day there would have been no one at Upleigh when his son departed. Both the cook and the maid, he would have stated, would have been at their mothers' homes. And this might have produced another breast-shaking spasm from Mrs. Sheringham. And the visiting policeman might have thought that he had asked questions enough, and put away his notebook.

But she, Jane Fairchild, would not have to answer any questions. Why should she? She was only the maid at Beechwood, not even at Upleigh. She had simply ridden off on her bicycle, and gone nowhere near, as it happened, the scene of the accident (though Mr. Niven might have thought that was why she had gone pale). Then she had returned, somewhat early.

And she had never heard—it was a never-spoken fact—as she wandered naked round that house any distant "crump." Would there have been a detectable "crump"? And she had never seen, in so far as she'd looked from any window, any smudge in that blue sky.

Though she had heard the telephone ring.

MR. NIVEN DIDN'T actually take hold of her. Not then. And she didn't faint, even if she had gone pale.

He repeated, "I'm so sorry, Jane, I'm so sorry to have to tell you this."

Why did it seem, at that complexion-changing moment, that she might have been someone else? It was an expression: "not to be yourself." Why did it seem that she might have been

Emma Hobday? Or that she might have been Mr. Niven's own daughter (though Mr. Niven didn't have one), who was also Emma Hobday. That Mr. Niven was, himself, Mr. Hobday. That the characters in this story had all been jumbled up.

Why did it seem that Mr. Niven was projecting onto her a whole confusion of scenes that she might have been in, but wasn't? She was only the maid—and, temporarily, not even that. Why did it seem that this day and its now terrible meaning—it wasn't Mothering Sunday any more at all—had blurred the usual order of things between herself and Mr. Niven?

He might have been speaking to his wife.

"Jane. Jane, I have left Clarissa—Mrs. Niven—with the others. In Henley. She felt she might be of better—service—there. Of course Emma—Miss Hobday—will drive to be with them. If she is able to. There was the question of whether they might all drive to her—to Bollingford. She is in Bollingford. Did I explain that? Or whether they might all drive to be at the Hobdays'. There is the question, Jane, of where everyone——ought to be. But I thought I should be here, Jane. I thought I should be here to . . ."

"Yes, Mr. Niven?"

"To go to Upleigh."

"Upleigh?"

"Yes. I stopped here first to use the telephone. I have just done so. I was just leaving. I have spoken to Clar——to Mrs. Niven. They are still at Henley. But they have decided to meet Miss Hobday——at the Hobdays'. That is the decision. I think that is the best plan. Miss Hobday must come first. Mr. and Mrs. Sheringham do not wish to return yet to Upleigh. Not yet. You can understand. I shall drive to the Hobdays' myself later. I am glad——I mean I am sorry——to be able to explain all this to you. But, Jane, you are back early——?"

"I thought, sir——it doesn't matter now——I might just come back here and read my book for a bit."

"Your book?"

"Yes."

"Well, if you—— I mustn't——"

"It doesn't matter, Mr. Niven. My book doesn't matter."

"Someone must inform the staff at Upleigh, you see. Mr. Sheringham has told me that your—opposite number—is called Ethel. And the cook is called Iris."

"But—"

"Yes, I know, they have gone to their families. Like Milly. But they must be made aware as soon as possible of the—circumstances. Mr. and Mrs. Sheringham told me—oh good God—that Paul drove them both to the station this morning, but they will return separately. This—Ethel—most likely first. So I must go to Upleigh, you see, to await her. To inform her."

"Not the station, sir?"

Had she gone pale twice?

"That might not be the best place for such a purpose. In any case—how can I put this, Jane?"

"Put what, sir?"

"I feel that someone must—ascertain the situation at Upleigh in any case. I mean the situation as Mister Paul would have left it."

"But—"

"Yes, of course, he would simply have left the house. Good God, he was going to be brushing up on his law apparently. Yes, he would simply have left the house. There is no situation. But I feel—someone should check the situation. To prepare the Sheringhams. I mean, to reassure them. They are not ready to return there yet. They feel they should be with Miss Hobday. But you can imagine, Jane, you can imagine. The state of their— I offered to do what I have just told you. To make sure of things at Upleigh. They said that when he—when Mister Paul—left, and as the house would have been empty, he would have left a key, under a piece of stone—a stone pineapple, they said. Mrs. Sheringham said it was a stone pineapple. By the front porch. So—"

"So—?"

"I must drive to Upleigh. To wait for this Ethel. And to ascertain—"

Mr. Niven did not seem entirely ready for the task he had plainly volunteered for. He cleared his troubled throat.

"Jane—may I ask you something?"

"Ask me what, Mr. Niven?"

She was still gripping the handlebars of the

bicycle. She realised she was even squeezing its brake levers, though she was standing, quite still, beside it.

"If you would accompany me."

"Go with you, sir?"

"Of course, I understand it is still *your* day. If you wish, Jane, if you wish just to read your book—"

"*Your* book, Mr. Niven." She had no idea why she corrected him.

"Of course."

A brief contortion crossed his face, as if the beginning of a smile had turned into something else.

Was he going to sob? This wasn't his son. He was only an entangled neighbour.

"Yes, sir. I will go with you."

"I appreciate that, Jane. That is very good of you. I don't suppose you have ever been inside Upleigh House—"

"Would you mind, Mr. Niven, if I went in first and had a glass of water?"

"Yes—of course. Forgive me. This is all such a shock. And you have been cycling around all day! Yes, yes, of course, you will need to collect yourself, refresh yourself. Forgive me. I will be here, Jane, by the car, when you are ready."

AND PERHAPS that five minutes or so made all the difference. And when had it ever happened before: Mr. Niven waiting for *her*? Even standing by the car, when she reappeared, with its leather-lined door opened for her. She thought again of Ethel and Iris.

Inside the house—inside another empty house—her face had momentarily flooded, before she drenched it anyway with cold water. She might even have stifled a scream.

They drove to Upleigh. It was not a long drive at all. But he drove very slowly and carefully, as if to some appointment he might have wished not to be keeping. They found it hard to speak. Yes, she felt like Ethel. She might have been Ethel.

And as it happened, Ethel was ahead of them. The docile and dutiful Ethel had decided, as if unequipped for her day of freedom, to return in time even to make the Sheringhams their tea, should they themselves be back early enough to require it. Her "day" with her mother must have been a matter of just a couple of hours, and perhaps, for her own reasons, she had preferred not to stretch it out any longer. She would have alighted from the 3:42, then simply walked. It was only a mile or so. There were shortcuts through fields. The sun would have been turning a deeper gold. Primroses peeping, rabbits hopping. It would have taken the agile Ethel maybe twenty minutes. And they might have been the best twenty minutes of her day.

Even as they drove up the Upleigh drive, between the limes, she had seen the tell-tale sign: the upstairs window. Tell-tale only to her. It was closed now. Someone had closed it. Who else but Ethel? Ethel had been in the bedroom and closed the window.

And so she'd gasped—audibly to Mr. Niven— as they still drove up the drive. And Mr. Niven had taken it perhaps as a general gasp of distress, since they were both no doubt thinking—if in different ways—of how Paul Sheringham had driven down this very drive only hours ago in the opposite direction. For the last time. So Mr. Niven had said needlessly, "Yes, it's terrible, Jane."

And it *was* a gasp of distress, but it contained a small gasp of relief. And she otherwise betrayed nothing.

The sun was now off the front of the house and the gravel. When they got out of the car there was even a distinct chill in the air after the earlier heat of midday. And while Mr. Niven began looking for "this pineapple thing" and while she restrained herself from pointing at it or saying anything, Ethel suddenly opened the door—as she naturally would, since it seemed that there were visitors. She might even have thought, hearing the car from within, that it was Mr. and Mrs. Sheringham returning. But there she was on the porch suddenly, with a surprising air of being in charge of—of guarding—the whole edifice of Upleigh.

And as she watched Ethel open the door she naturally thought of when she had last seen it being opened.

"MR. NIVEN——?" Ethel had mustered, with a mixture of surprise and composure which didn't begin to embrace the puzzle of why Mr. Niven was there with Jane What-was-her-name, the maid from Beechwood.

Were all maids being offered rides today?

And Mr. Niven said, "You are Ethel, aren't you?" Which was also puzzling.

So there had been no need to wait for Ethel. She struggled, later, to imagine what that might have been like. And the whole procedure of informing Ethel took place at the front porch. Since Ethel plainly wouldn't be told to go in and sit down, not by Mr. Niven who wasn't her own master, even though it was clear from his manner that something really awful might be about to be uttered. And was that Beechwood girl supposed to be coming inside and sitting down too?

Ethel, in fact, suddenly changed. Or perhaps her true Ethelness appeared. She would never know if her (and even Paul Sheringham's) whole conception of Ethel had been mistaken from the beginning.

Ethel's eyes, even as Mr. Niven was grappling with words again, had suddenly bored into her own as if she, Ethel Bligh, knew everything. Though equally they might have been saying, just as unswervingly, "We maidservants have to stick together, don't we, and know our place in the world?"

Her look went a lot further anyway than a mere bewildered, "And what are *you* doing here? What are you doing consorting with your master?"

Behind Ethel, she could just make out, through the vestibule and the shadows of the hall, the table and the bowl with the white clusters of orchids. It was somehow incredible that they should still be there.

"I have some distressing news, Ethel," Mr. Niven began. "If I may call you Ethel?"

"Yes, sir."

And so Ethel was informed. And stood there, like an unbudging defender on the front porch, as if she were fully prepared, now so much harm had apparently come to this house, to prevent any further assaults upon it. Mr. Niven, who was still on the gravel below, seemed to cower before her sudden authority.

"Then it is just as well, Mr. Niven, I came back early, so I can be of assistance. I must have known in my bones something was wrong. That I might be needed. Mr. and Mrs. Sheringham—they must be quite beside themselves. They must be in such a state, again." Ethel had said that deliberate "again." "I will be here for them when they return. I will inform Cook when she returns. I will take—I will make, if required—any telephone calls."

"Ethel—"

But Ethel had carried on, perhaps in rare defiance, for her, of the speak-when-spoken-to rule.

"I have already tidied around. I have tidied Mister Paul's room—"

"That is just the point, Ethel."

"The point, Mr. Niven?"

"I need to ask you— I am here to ascertain—" Mr. Niven floundered. "Did you find anything, in Mister Paul's room?"

"Anything? I don't know what you mean, Mr. Niven."

"Like—a note, Ethel. Anything written."

"No, sir. I did not find anything written. And I would not have read it if I had, sir." Ethel almost looked as if her next words might have been a snappy, "Would that be all, sir?" Or even a "And what business would that be of yours?"

"Then— That is all right, Ethel. That is all—all right."

"Are *you* all right, sir? Would you be requiring a cup of tea or anything?"

"No, thank you, Ethel. Are *you* all right? Would you require—our company? Or Jane here's company?"

That was a possibility she, the Beechwood maid, hadn't been prepared for and she waited, surrenderingly, for Ethel's grasping of the initiative.

"No, sir. I can manage, thank you."

But she had said it not looking at Mr. Niven, but squarely, unwaveringly at her "opposite number."

And her look was like the look of the sternest and most forgiving of parents.

SO, SHE WOULD NEVER know many things. But she knew now that, certainly by the time the Sheringhams returned, Ethel would have thoroughly "tidied up" Mister Paul's room. The flung-aside trousers, the bedclothes. The sheets would have been replaced (though no one, Ethel must later have reflected on this, was going to sleep in them), the removed ones bundled into the laundry basket, waiting for Monday's copper. The kitchen table—a simple kindness to Cook Iris—would have been cleared and cleaned. And everything returned to as it should be. Even though everything was different.

And Ethel would one day find her way into another minor (not so minor) character—in *If the Truth Be Known*. She would be transmuted and (though only the author would know) honoured by fiction. She would not be called Ethel (she would be called Edith) or be anything like Ethel, or even be a maid, but she would be one of those characters who exist, seemingly, on the periphery of things and yet know everything. And she would be one of those characters whose real "character" goes for most of the time unsuspected and unperceived. But that was a general truth she, the author, would know by then to apply to the creation of character in fiction, as it was a general truth about life and people.

But she would never know exactly how much Ethel had known all along. And she would never know what Ethel did or thought or imagined or felt when she was left alone again in that house in the interval before the Sheringhams (and Cook Iris) returned, and even, in time, the police appeared, just for some routine questions.

She would hardly have composed a thank-you note to her mother.

THEY DROVE BACK. The sun was dipping and turning orange. The afternoon was waning. And crispening. It was only March. Ethel would light fires too, no doubt, among her other tasks. The right thing to do in the circumstances, keep the home fires burning. Just as she herself would do soon, when she became a maid again at Beechwood.

What was she now, for the time being?

Mr. Niven said, after a long silence, "I'm sorry to have kept you from your reading, Jane. I'm so sorry to have used up your time. What is the book at present? I forget."

"It's all right, sir. It doesn't matter."

She was sitting beside him in the front seat, where, when her husband drove, Mrs. Niven would sit. She was trying very hard not to weep, to hold herself together.

If only Mr. Niven might say, "You must take the evening off. You must take a long hot bath." But maids never took long hot baths or were given unscheduled evenings off, especially when they had had the day off anyway. In a little while she would have to resume her duties. She would have to be at least as strong as Ethel.

The gathering evening, the apricot light, the gauzy green-gold world, was impossibly beautiful.

After another long silence he said, "That's all five of them, Jane."

She knew what he meant. She knew exactly what he meant. But she said, "Yes, sir," in the way that maids simply mouth those words in general concurrence with everything.

Then, when they'd turned into the sweep in front of Beechwood and he'd switched off the engine he suddenly leant across to her and, like a child, wept—blubbed—even pressed his head, his face to her breasts, so that she thought of when she'd pressed them—had it been only this afternoon?—to the opened pages of a book. "I'm so sorry, Jane, I'm so sorry," he said, even as his face remained where it was. And she said, involuntarily cradling the back of his head, "That's quite all right, Mr. Niven, that's quite all right."

THE BOOK WAS called *Youth*—the book she might have read on the bench in the garden, or might have mentioned to Mr. Niven when he'd asked. She might have just uttered the odd word "youth."

Or rather it was called *Youth, a Narrative; and Two Other Stories*, a clumsy, unexciting mishmash of a title. It was the only book by Joseph Conrad in the Beechwood library, and the narrative called *Youth* was the first thing in it and a good place anyway to start, since, as she would come to know, it was loosely based on Conrad's own early experiences and on his first encounter (she would come to know that he wrote about it often) with a thing—a vision, a promise, a fact, an illusion—called "the East."

It was anyway what, on that Mothering Sunday, she'd only just begun, and if her day had gone differently, if the telephone hadn't rung, she might quite easily have finished it in some sunny corner of Berkshire or even in the Beechwood garden. She might even have got on to the *Other Stories*. One of them was called "Heart of Darkness" and as it turned out (her Mothering Sunday having turned out as it did) it was a long time before she got round to that story, even though she knew she had discovered in Joseph Conrad someone important. It was the forbidding title perhaps.

She knew that Conrad was different from anything else she had read, but she could sense that there were things she might not be ready for. It was a little like reading *Treasure Island* and *Kidnapped* but not wanting yet to read *Dr. Jekyll and Mr. Hyde*.

She quite liked the word "narrative," it was a sober, dependable-sounding word, but she didn't see why the one thing should be called a narrative and the other things just stories. The word she most liked in those days was "tale"—and she was glad to find out that Conrad often preferred it too. There was something more enticing about calling something a tale rather than a story, but this had to do, perhaps, with the suggestion that it might not be wholly truthful, it might have a larger element of invention.

About all these words—"tale," "story," even "narrative"—there was a sort of question, always hovering in the background, of truth, and it might be hard to say how much truth went with each. There was also the word "fiction"— one day this would be the very thing she dealt in—which could seem almost totally dismissive of truth. A complete fiction! Yet something that was clearly and completely fiction could also contain—this was the nub and the mystery of the matter—truth. When she had read all three of them, she felt she could say *Dr. Jekyll and Mr. Hyde* was more truthful than *Treasure Island* or *Kidnapped.* Though some people might say it was the weirdest and certainly the most frightening of the lot.

"Telling tales": it could have the sense of concocting downright lies. Like "spinning yarns." It seemed in fact that "yarn" might be the best word for those adventure books she'd been first drawn to in the library at Beechwood, and to have questioned whether those books were truthful would have been pointless. They were yarns. In the word "yarn" itself there was a salty tang of men and the sea. And so many of those "boys' books" she read had involved, one way or another, going to sea—a voyage, an unknown land—as if that was the essence of adventure and what every boy wanted to do. And here was Joseph Conrad who seemed to have been just one of those boys.

And she liked the word "youth." Or rather she was challenged by it, because it wasn't in any obvious way like the title of a tale, story or narrative—or adventure. It seemed more like just an idea. Yet when she had first flipped through the pages of *Youth* in the Beechwood library it had seemed to be full of all that seafaring, yarny stuff she was already familiar with. Perhaps it was what one of the Niven boys, or by then young men, had thought too, though it was obvious he hadn't got very far with the book, if he'd read it at all. Unlike other books in the revolving bookcase, it still looked clean and new. It even bore an inscription, in dark-blue ink,

"J. Niven, Oct. 1915," that looked fresh enough to have been written yesterday. And maybe that was another reason why she picked it out.

Conrad, she soon felt, might be generally called a "challenging author." "Heart of Darkness" . . . Maybe J. Niven had thought this too. "Challenging author" was not yet part of her writer-judging vocabulary and certainly not a phrase she could imagine one day being applied to herself. She would take it, when it was, as a complimentary phrase, but of course there were people who used it adversely. It was another way of saying "off-putting." Well, that was their bloody problem.

"CONRAD," she would say, when answering another of those repeated and bothersome questions. "Oh Conrad—he was the one." As if she were talking about someone she had met. Which in a sense she had.

"Oh Conrad, I used to love all that seafaring stuff."

"But a man's author, don't you think?"

"And your point is . . . ?"

The other reason why she liked the word "youth" was of course that it was what she had—then. She was "a youth." Although there was a way in which "youth," like "yarn," had a strongly masculine bias to it. A man could be a "youth," but a woman? But then everything had a masculine bias in 1924.

There was in any case a question—and the word "youth" seemed to have a rubbery quality to it to accommodate this—about where youth began and where it turned into something else. But, surely, still at twenty-two. In 1924 even the century was still in its youth . . . Though, in fact, that wasn't the case at all. Youth—great swathes of it—was just what the century had lost.

And, yes, of course, by 1924 Conrad was arguably outmoded, already behind the times. Sailing ships? The exotic East? Didn't he know what had happened to the world?

BUT HE WAS truly the one. On the night of Mothering Sunday 1924, when, for good reasons, she was utterly unable to sleep or rest, she picked up again Joseph Conrad's *Youth*. What else could she do? Cry? And cry again? In her little plank of a bed. People read books, didn't they, to get away from themselves, to escape the troubles of their lives?

And it was and it wasn't an adventure story. It was different, it had something special. It was about five crusty old men sitting round a table—yarning—who had done different things with their lives, but had all once been at sea, in their youth. She could see the men at the table, see their lined faces. One of them was called Marlow and it was he who told his story. It wasn't really an adventure story at all. It was about a dumpy old ship that was always having bad luck, never getting far from murky home waters, but which one day, at the end of the story, which was also a sort of beginning, finally makes it to—the East.

WHEN SHE HAD finished *Youth and Other Stories*, even managing to read "Heart of Darkness"—which was indeed challenging and truly like nothing else she had read—she knew she had to get more Conrad, and so she'd written to a bookshop in Reading which sent books by post. She had the half-crown still that Mr. Niven had given her, not to mention other half-crowns put by. She could buy a postal order in the village. And dealing with a bookshop in this enterprising way perhaps even made her think: A bookshop, a bookshop . . .

She bought a book called *Lord Jim*, which was not unlike *Youth*, but much longer—and challenging. It was called a "tale." It involved that man Marlow again, and it was tempting to think that Marlow was really Conrad in disguise. Then she bought a book called *The Secret Agent*, which was quite different, since it wasn't set in the East or to do with ships, but set in the grubby streets of London, though it still had that feeling of entering unknown and possibly dangerous territory which, if she'd had the word, she might have called "Conradian."

By then she'd think that Conrad himself must be a sort of secret agent, slipping between worlds. And much later she'd think and sometimes say that all writers are secret agents. But perhaps the truth was—though she wouldn't say this—that we are all secret agents, that's what we are.

Anyway, by the time she'd read *The Secret Agent*, and foolish as it might have been, she had formed her own secret wish to become a writer. And she was not unused to having secrets.

It wasn't his real name—Conrad—she found out, since he was really Polish. So he had a name a little like hers. It wasn't a pen name either, it was just his "English" name. But the remarkable, the truly astonishing thing about Joseph Conrad was that in order to write all his books, he hadn't just had to learn how to write, but to write in a *whole new language*. That was almost unbelievable. It was like crossing some impossible—impassable—barrier, and she felt that perhaps that was the greater thing, the greater achievement and truer adventure, greater even than going on all those voyages in his youth, more thrilling even than reaching the East.

And it was what she would have to do to become a writer: cross an impossible barrier. And she too, she would come to understand this, would have to find a language, even though she

had a language, since finding a language, finding *the* language—that was what, she would
come to understand, writing really was. But she
would seldom say these things in interviews
either. They were too near the bone.

"Conrad, oh yes—he had something special."
As if she might have been talking about some
old lover.

And, if the truth be known, in her last months
at Beechwood and before she "went to Oxford"
it became a thrill for her to know that Joseph
Conrad, who'd been born in Poland and had
sailed the seas, was actually alive then, somewhere not so far away, in the folds of England. A
thrill that couldn't last long, though she'd been
alive to know it, because one morning in August
1924—it was like a sudden personal shock—
she'd read in the paper, before reflattening it and
putting it on Mr. Niven's breakfast table, that
Joseph Conrad had died.

And, if the truth be known (though she would
never say this, in interviews or to anyone), all
the pictures she'd got to see of Joseph Conrad—
the later Conrad—had made her fall in love

with him. The gravity, the beard, the expression in his eyes as if he were seeing something far off that was also deep inside. She had even sometimes imagined what it might be like to lie in bed with Conrad, just to lie beside him, not speaking, a naked, ageing Conrad, both of them looking up and watching the smoke from their cigarettes rising, mingling under the ceiling, as if the smoke held some truth greater than either of them could find words for.

The first sigh of the East on my face. That I can never forget.

SHE WOULD BECOME a writer. She would write books. She would write nineteen novels. She would even become a "modern writer." Though how long do you remain "modern"? It was like the word "youth." And was that what writing was about anyway: modernity? She would know times and changes, and write about them. She would live to be over ninety, nearly a hundred, and in her later years when she developed a definite mischievous streak and when she was wheeled out yet again—"Jane Fairchild at Eighty," "Jane Fairchild at Ninety"—she would mention the names of writers of the past as if, once upon a time, they had actually been her friends.

All the scenes. All the real ones and all the ones in books. And all the ones that were somehow in-between, because they were only what you could picture and imagine of real people. Like trying to picture her mother. Or only what you could suppose might have been true, if things had turned out differently, once, long ago. She might have gone with him, it might somehow have been magically arranged, to stand, pressed close to him, by the rail, in the chill of the dawn, as the sun unfurled great fiery carpets across the downs and as Fandango drew close, nostrils flaring and steaming, hooves pounding. She might have understood it and known it for ever. The fourth leg? The fourth leg was hers.

She would tell in her books many stories. She would even begin to tell, in her later careless years, stories about her own life, in such a way that you could never quite know if they were true or made up. But there was one story she would never tell. On some things she would be as impeccably silent as Ethel (who became Edith after all) proved to be. As silent as, she supposed, Joseph Conrad, for all his story-telling genius, would have been about some things, lying there beside her like some wonderful hollow husk of a man.

Telling stories, telling tales. Always the implication that you were trading in lies. But for her it would always be the task of getting to the quick, the heart, the nub, the pith: the trade of truth-telling. It had been Donald's task too, in his way. Poor Donald, taken away from her forty, fifty years ago.

Enough of this interview claptrap and chi-canery. So what was it then exactly, this truth-telling? They would always want even the explanation explained! And any writer worth her salt would lead them on, tease them, lead them up the garden path. Wasn't it bloody obvious? It was about being true to the very stuff of life, it was about trying to capture, though you never could, the very feel of being alive. It was about finding a language. And it was about being true to the fact, the one thing only followed from the other, that many things in life—oh so many more than we think—can never be explained at all.

ENGLAND AND OTHER STORIES

In these beautifully crafted stories, Graham Swift—author of the Booker Prize–winning *Last Orders*—presents a vision of England that is both a crucible of history and a maze of contemporary confusions. Moving from the seventeenth century to the present day, from world-shaking events to domestic dramas and frequently mixing tragedy with comedy, *England and Other Stories* is bound together by an underlying instinct for the story of us all: an evocation of that mysterious thing, a nation, enriched by a clear-eyed compassion for how human individuals find or lose their way in the nationless territory of birth, growing up, sex, aging, and death.

Fiction

WISH YOU WERE HERE

On an autumn day in 2006, on the Isle of Wight, Jack Luxton—once a Devon farmer, now the proprietor of a seaside caravan park—receives the news that his brother, Tom, not seen for years, has been killed in combat in Iraq. For Jack and his wife, Ellie, this will have unexpected, far-reaching effects. For Jack in particular it means a crucial journey: to receive his brother's remains and to confront his most secret, troubling memories. A hauntingly intimate, deeply compassionate story about things that touch and test our human core, *Wish You Were Here* also looks, inevitably, to a wider, afflicted world. Moving toward a fiercely suspenseful climax, it brilliantly transforms the stuff of headlines into a heart-wrenching personal truth.

Fiction

MAKING AN ELEPHANT
Writing from Within

In his first-ever work of nonfiction, Graham Swift—
Booker Prize–winning author of *Waterland* and *Last
Orders*—gives us a highly personal book: a singular
and open-spirited account of a writer's life. Here Kazuo
Ishiguro advises on how to choose a guitar; Salman Rushdie
arrives for Christmas under guard; Caryl Phillips shares
a beer with the author at a nightclub in Toronto. There
are private moments with Swift's father and with his own
younger self, as well as musings—on history, memory, and
imagination—that illuminate his work. As generous in its
scope as it is acute in its observations, *Making an Elephant*
brings together a richly varied selection of essays, portraits,
poetry and interviews, full of insights into Swift's passions
and motivations, and wise about the friends, family, and
other writers who have mattered to him over the years.

Memoir

ALSO AVAILABLE

Ever After
Last Orders
Learning to Swim
The Light of Day
Out of This World
Shuttlecock
The Sweet-Shop Owner
Tomorrow
Waterland

VINTAGE INTERNATIONAL
Available wherever books are sold.
www.vintagebooks.com